The Cowboy and His Valentine

His Valentine

Cowboys of Rock Springs, Texas #2

Kaci M. Rose

Five Little Roses Publishing

Copyright

Book Cover By: **Sarah Kil Creative Studio**
Editing By: Debbe @ **On The Page, Author
and PA Services**

Blurb

Love is in the air, and Cupid's arrows are flying in Rock Springs, Texas!

Maggie

As a newcomer to Rock Springs, I'm eager to move out from under the thumb of my conservative parents and discover who I am. Helping my sister out, at the town's annual Sweetheart Dance, seems like a great place to start. I don't believe in the silly legend about soulmates finding each other at the event, until I meet Nick. He's even more delicious than the BBQ he cooks, but the intense heat he brings doesn't stop at the kitchen door. Unsure if I'm ready to be struck by Cupid's Arrow, I pull back. Candy and flowers will have to wait, because I need to discover who I am first.

Nick

Between the work I do at the restaurant and my family's ranch, my life is a busy whirlwind. But everything slowed to crystal clear clarity, the second I locked eyes with Maggie. Rock Spring legend states that the person you attend your first Sweetheart Dance with is your soulmate, and I believe that with my whole heart. Now, I'm determined to walk under that balloon arch with her on my arm. I see her hesitating at the sizzling chemistry between us. Can I win her over in time to call her my valentine?

Come meet the small town of Rock Springs, Texas with a family that has your back, a town that knows your business, and men who love with everything they have.

Dedication

To the coffee that kept me going, and the kids
that call me mommy.

Contents

Get Free Books!

Would you like some free cowboy books?
**If you join Kaci M. Rose's Newsletter you
get books and bonus epilogues free!
Join Kaci M. Rose's newsletter and get
your free books!**
https://www.kacirose.com/KMR-Newsletter

Now on to the story!

Chapter 1

Maggie

Who knew a pair of jeans could make someone so happy? I think it's a great way to start the New Year. For years, my parents insisted my sister and I wear dresses and skirts, but no pants. At the time, I had no problem with it.

Then, my sister got married, and she married into a different kind of family than any of us would have ever expected. They not only welcomed Ella with open arms but me and my whole family as well. So much so, that we moved from our small town of Mountain Gap, Tennessee to the even smaller town of Rock Springs, Texas to be around them and my sister.

The more time I spent on the ranch, the more I loved it. But dresses and skirts just weren't practical, so I talked to my parents about wearing jeans. I know I didn't need their permission. I'm twenty-five years old after all, but I'm really close with my parents and still live with them, so their approval made things easier.

So today, I stand in WJ's, my sister Ella and her husband's bar turned family restaurant, in jeans. It's also the New Year's Eve party, and I'm doing something else for myself. I'm here taking pictures of the couples. It's my first paid photography gig, even if it was my sister who booked me.

That's the next battle I have with my parents. I want to start my own photography business, and possibly, move out and live on my own. I know they will support the photography business, but it's the moving out on my own they won't be a fan of. They are very conservative, and would rather I stay home until I married.

Being that I have no marriage prospects and don't plan to any time soon, I'd really like to live my life and not feel like it's on hold until some man comes into it. Though, I guess I should phrase it a bit better than that to my parents.

"Oh, our turn! Make the baby bump look good!" Megan sequels, as she and her husband, Hunter, step up to get their photo taken. She's one of Ella's sister-in-laws, and now part of my family, too.

She barely has a baby bump and is only about sixteen weeks, but she swears everyone can tell now. She stands sideways with Hunter behind her, as they both cradle her bump. It's just so sweet, and with some strategic moves, I get the bump to stand out, while still making them both look like the cutest couple ever.

I show them the photos on the computer I have set up and soak in their huge smiles.

"Oh, Maggie, you're amazing. I love this, and I can't wait to frame it for our room!"

"Now, let me spin you around the dance floor, before you get too tired to dance with me," Hunter says, as he starts moving her towards the dance floor.

With a break in photos, I take in the bar. I had such a blast decorating it with Ella. We spent a day taking down all the Christmas decorations and then putting up all the black and gold New Year's ones.

I shiver, as I think of that day. I took a walk to get some fresh air and ran into Nick. He asked me out, and I turned him down. Dating just isn't in the cards for me right now, but I still think of his response.

"I'm not giving up so easily, Maggie. You can count on it."

It's all I've been able to think about, and I've decided that I don't want him to give up. I just don't know how anything between us will work. I know my parents want me to go about it as Ella did with a courtship.

Courtship means very minimal physical contact, and you always have a chaperone with you. Ella didn't have her first kiss, until her wedding night. I'm not sure that's how I see myself, finding my future husband.

I've thought about dating, like I've seen it on TV, with kissing on the first date, living together before marriage, and having sex so early on. I'm not sure that's right for me either. There has to be an option in between, and there has to be a guy out there who is okay with it.

Nick's face floats through my mind again, and it's almost like I conjured him up, as he steps out of the kitchen and takes a look around. Nick is an amazing chef. He's won multiple awards for his food, but most recently, would be the BBQ Championship Award he won in Dallas.

It was featured on national TV, and then, another TV show came and did a special on WJ's, and it brought in some business for the town. Nick could work in a huge kitchen in Dallas, Las Vegas, or even New York City, but he chooses to stay here. He and Jason went to school together and are best friends, so I know he's loyal to him, which means a lot.

He has those cowboy muscles and a tan that mixes with his dark brown hair that's just long enough to have a slight curl to it. He wears a very short beard that looks almost like a perfectly styled five o'clock shadow. I've never been a fan of beards on men, but Nick's is extremely sexy, and it definitely changed my mind on the matter.

His eyes land on mine, and his whole face lights up, as he starts making his way across the room.

Ten. Nine. Eight.

I barely hear the New Year's countdown going on because it's like his eyes are holding me in a trance. When he's right in front of me, the rest of the room fades away.

Seven. Six. Five.

He places a hand on my hip, and my brain shuts down. I should pull back. I should walk off, but all I can think about are the sparks of heat, where his hands are touching me.

Four. Three.

He takes a step closer, and his eyes scan my face. The soft look in them does me in. My eyes land on his lips. He isn't going to kiss me, right? Surely, it will be just a kiss on the forehead.

Two. One.

In the next instant, his lips are on mine, and they are soft and warm. I kiss him back without thought because I *want* to kiss him. His hand tangles in my hair and pulls me closer, making me gasp. He slides his tongue into my mouth, and the second his tongue touches mine, reality crashes around me.

I push him away, and the shock registers on his face, as I take a step back. I bring a hand up to my lips, and they feel like they're on fire.

My first kiss.

Oh God, what have I done?

"Maggie," Nicks says, as I rush by him, scanning the crowd for someone, anyone, and the first person I find is my brother, Royce, talking to Anna Mae. He sees me before I fully make my way to him, and his face drops.

"What's wrong?" He rushes over with concern on his face.

"Please, take me home, Royce. Please." I plead.

"Of course." He slides an arm around my waist and leads me to the door, no questions asked.

Before I step through the door, I turn my head and catch a glimpse of Jason, rushing towards Nick, his face full of rage. I guess, he saw what happened. Then, there's Nick, watching me with the saddest look on his face.

As soon as the door closes behind me, I start crying. One of the many things I like about Royce is he doesn't pry. He just helps me into his truck and makes sure I'm buckled up, before closing the door and heading to his side to get in.

As we pull out of the parking lot, he looks over at me, but still doesn't ask questions.

"I'm sorry," I mumble. I hate that I pulled him away from Anna Mae. He's been trying to get her to go out with him for months, but she keeps putting him off. I know they were having a good time tonight, and they even took a photo together. I instantly feel guilty for ruining the night for him.

"Don't be, Maggie. There isn't anything I wouldn't do for you and Ella. Do you want to talk about it?" He asks gently.

"Not yet, but I promise I will, when I'm ready," I tell him.

He nods because that's enough for him. He turns the radio on for background noise, as we drive back out to the ranch. Mom, Dad, Royce, and I are staying in the old family house on Sage's side of the ranch until we find a place in town. Ella and Sage keep finding ways to keep us here longer, which is just fine by me.

I stare out the window, watching the north Texas landscape of mostly flat ranch land go by, as the night flashes through my head.

Nick kissed me.

Nick *kissed* me, and I liked it.

I don't know how I pictured my first kiss. For a while, it was on my wedding day, but over the last few years, I pictured something more. A declaration of *'I love you'* followed by a passionate kiss. Maybe, it would be after he asked me to marry him.

Never once did I think my first kiss would be at the stroke of midnight in a bar before I had even been on a first date with the guy.

But this isn't just any guy. *It's Nick.*

Nick who makes my heartbeat fast by just being in the same room. Nick who can look at me and make me feel like the most beautiful girl in the world. Nick who has asked me out and told me he won't stop fighting for me.

"I'm not giving up so easy, Maggie. You can count on it."

Those words run through my head again. I only admitted to myself this evening that I didn't want him to give up. I want him to prove to me that he wants me and that I'm worth it. I want him to be the one who is okay with my crazy dating rules, and okay with me figuring them out as we go. *I want it to be him.*

I bring my hand up to my lips again. I can still feel his lips on mine. Why did that one kiss shock me so much? I wanted to kiss him. I still do, but when his tongue touched mine, it was a feeling I wasn't expecting. My body wanted him in a whole new way. I was so turned on in the middle of a crowded bar, that I didn't know what to do.

I know I'm going to have to talk to him. I'm also going to have to explain and apologize for whatever lashing Jason is giving him right now.

I'm going to have to explain to Royce, Ella, and Jason. They will insist I talk to my parents as well. I know everyone at the ranch is there for me if I need them.

The problem is I have no idea how to explain what happened. Nick kissed me, and I liked it, but I pushed him away and hurt us both. Why?

I'm not sure. Part of me was waiting for my parents to yell and ground me, like a little girl, knowing they would be disappointed in me. Another part was upset I wasn't in control and deciding that moment would be my first kiss.

We pull into the ranch and pass the main house to our place a bit further down from the barn.

Royce, ever the gentleman, helps me from the truck and into the house. I sit in the chair by the fireplace, and Royce places a blanket over my shoulders before he starts to make a fire.

Once the fire is roaring, he stands back up and looks at me.

"What do you need?" He asks me.

"Will you ask Jason, Ella, Mom, and Dad to come home? I know it's late, but I'd rather have this conversation only once, and I know I won't be able to sleep until I do."

"Of course," he says, as he pulls out his phone and steps into the kitchen to make the calls.

I stare at the fire in the fireplace that matches the one, roaring inside of me, and dreading the conversation ahead.

Chapter 2

Nick

"What the fuck was that?" Jason roars at me.

I'm still so numb that I don't move. I can't tear my eyes off the door Maggie just disappeared out of with her brother. I can still feel her warm, soft lips on mine. Holy shit, I kissed Maggie. That was the hottest kiss I've ever had, and it just reaffirms I was right.

Maggie is mine, and I will wait as long as she needs and fight as hard as I have to, proving it to her. That kiss was unlike anything I've ever felt, and I know she felt it too because I could see it in her eyes. Maybe, that's what scared her so much?

I picture her face just before the kiss. Her long, blonde hair in stunning waves over her shoulder, and just enough makeup to make her dark brown eyes pop. Her eyes fell to my lips, and her tongue darted out to wet her full lips, and I knew there was no way I could walk away and not kiss her. I know I'd do it all over again, too.

Before I can let that sink in, Jason is gripping my arm, as my eyes swing to his, and all I see is anger. This is what I saw on his face, when a football player who was dating his sister, Megan, was talking about how he took her to Grayson Field. That was the spot where guys would take their dates to cop a feel.

Her date said she was uptight when he tried to get into her pants, but he was going to ask her to prom to get *a piece of that sweet ass*. The guy never made it to prom, but instead, ended up with two black eyes, a broken arm, and two broken ribs.

When Jason's parents found out what he did, he was praised and treated like a king at home. The other guy's parents threatened to press charges until Jason's parents said they would counter with sexual assault. That scared the school, and those parents dropped it.

The rage on his face is very close to that day, and it's not something I've seen on him since. I'm not sure what happened, but I know I need to take Jason seriously.

"My office. Now." He grits out.

"Jason!" Ella, his wife, hisses. Ella is also Maggie's sister, so I know Jason is going to be protective of her, but I'm not sure why he's so upset. It was just a kiss.

I let him lead me to his office like I don't know the way. Like I haven't been working here for the last eight years, since I graduated culinary school. I don't care that all eyes seem to be on us either. I'd rather do this in his office than out on the floor.

I sit down on the couch, as the door slams behind me. Jason and I stare each other down, waiting for the other to speak. Well, this is a move we have done, since the day we met when we both thought the other was in the wrong. The first one to talk isn't Jason or me, it's Ella, who speaks and calms us both down.

"Jason, I don't think he understands what he did wrong." She whispers to him, as she puts her hand on his chest and his whole demeanor changes with just her touch. Even in the midst of the situation, I can't help being a little jealous. I want that in my life, and I want my soul mate, who can calm me with one touch.

He wraps his arms around her, burying his face in her hair, before looking back up at me. He's back to his calm, put together self. What the touch of the right woman can do.

"Why did you kiss her?" He asks me.

"It was New Year's, and everyone was kissing someone, so I took a chance," I tell him. I still don't see what I did wrong. Does he not want me dating his wife's sister? Does he not want me in his family? Does he think I'm not good enough for her?

"Maggie's family doesn't date like you do. They are more conservative and follow their religious beliefs." He says as he sits down, pulling Ella into his lap.

"What do you mean?" I never really paid much attention to the details of Jason and Ella's relationship. They moved fast, and I had just won the BBQ award, and there was a lot of PR I was doing for the bar in the wake of it. Then, there was the TV show that did a whole segment on us. By the time things settled down, they were married.

"They don't date. They court."

"What does that mean?" I ask.

"It means all dates are chaperoned, and our first kiss? Ella's first kiss? Was on our wedding day."

The blood drains from my face, and I actually feel it happening. That wasn't just our first kiss, it was Maggie's first kiss. I know she liked it, but when she looked away, it did look like her whole world was crashing around her, and I had no idea why.

Had she planned for her first kiss to be on her wedding day?

Shit.

"I see you're starting to get it now," Jason says.

"I have to make this right," I say without thinking, as my mind is already racing.

I will need to talk to her parents and take whatever they throw at me. Then, I will have to get on my knees and beg for forgiveness from Maggie, but I can start here and now with Jason and Ella.

"I didn't know. I swear I didn't. I'm so sorry, and I swear I'll make this right. Somehow, I will make this right." I say.

Ella leans over and whispers into Jason's ear, before kissing his cheek.

"Well, if you make it right with Maggie, then we'll be fine, okay?" Jason says.

I nod. It's all still sinking in. Jason and Ella step back out to say goodbye, as people start heading home.

I can't move. My mind is at war with my body, and my body is still on fire from that kiss. I can still feel her lips, dancing across mine. I can feel the moment her body gave in to the kiss, and also, the moment she pulled away.

It happened so fast that I didn't even get my head cleared quickly enough to ask what was wrong before she took off and made a beeline for her brother.

My mind is saying I have to beg for her forgiveness, but then, it says I should leave her alone. A girl like that, so innocent and pure, would never go for a guy like me. It can be a distant memory that she laughs at with her future husband.

A knife twists in my gut at the thought of her marrying some other guy. I stand up not sure what I need, but I know I can't sit here and think about this for the rest of the night.

"Hey, Royce called a family meeting. I'm guessing Maggie is going to get this in the open tonight. Ella's parents just left, and we're heading out now, so that means you're closing up." Jason comes up to me.

"Of course, no problem. I need the time to think anyway." I tell him.

"Listen, I'll do what damage control I can, but I can't make any promises."

"I know, and I appreciate whatever you can do."

"I was going to mention this earlier anyway. Can you be in early tomorrow, around noon? There's something I need to talk to you about before we open." He asks.

"Of course, I'll be here."

We had considered shutting down because the first was on a Friday. Since Friday and Saturday nights are our biggest nights of the week, we decided against it. Sage and Colt agreed to come in and help, so we could give the bar staff a break, but most of my kitchen staff volunteered to come in for the extra hours, so we will make do with what we have.

Before they head out, Ella comes over and hugs me. It's gentle and just what I needed right then.

"Don't give up on her. She isn't like me. She's a lot more independent, but a whole lot more stubborn. She's still figuring herself out, so be patient." Ella says.

I watch her and Jason walk out, and the last few customers follow behind them. I lock the doors, as the staff and I start the cleanup.

Ella will be in tomorrow with some of Jason's sisters to remove the decorations, so we just need to do a basic cleaning of the place, and then close down the bar and kitchen. As the staff starts with that, I close down the tills, and it takes me three times to count the money because my mind is everywhere, but where it needs to be.

We end up leaving around three a.m., and once I make sure everyone is safely to their cars, I get in my truck and take the first deep breath I have in hours.

My body is tired, but my mind is still racing. How can I make this right? This isn't a go get a dozen roses, and I'm so sorry I stole your first kiss you were saving for your husband kind of moment. Food doesn't even seem like a big enough gesture.

Jewelry, maybe? My mom always said my dad could buy his way out of a fight with jewelry. Hey, thanks for letting me steal your first kiss, and here's a diamond necklace. Ugh, it doesn't seem like a good idea either. I don't think there's a thing on this planet I could buy to fix this.

I pull into my place. *The house is mine.* I had it built when I moved back to Rock Springs, but it's on my parent's ranch, and I help out whenever I can. Over the winter, my dad likes to do repairs around the place, so next week, I'm helping him and my mom redecorate the guest room.

Well, it's my old room they are turning into a guest room, and I'm responsible for packing up the last of my things. I try to concentrate on what I need to do to help my parents, as I get ready for bed, but even that, barely takes my mind off of Maggie.

When I finally close my eyes, all I see is Maggie. I can feel her soft lips on mine, and I'm as hard as a rock. I won't do anything to fix that either, because it's my punishment for what I did to her.

I hope Jason has good news tomorrow. I could sure use something else to concentrate on until I figure out how to make this right.

Chapter 3

Maggie

Jason and Ella walk into the house just behind Mom and Dad. I haven't moved from my spot in front of the fire, and even with the heat coming off of it, I'm still numb.

"Maggie, baby, are you okay?" My mom sits down beside me, pulling me into her.

Dad sits on the edge of the couch closest to Mom like he's ready to jump to her aid the moment she needs it. Jason sits in the love seat and pulls Ella next to him. Royce crouches down in front of me and puts his hand on my knee.

"We're all here and on your side, Maggie, no matter what." Royce's voice is so soft, and I know he's got my back.

He protected Ella at every step with the whole Seth thing back home, while Jason and Ella were courting, so I know he'd do the same for me. The problem is in the whole time it took for everyone to get home I still haven't sorted out how I feel about the kiss. Much less, how I'm going to tell everyone.

I keep my eyes on the fire. It's easier than trying to make or avoid eye contact with anyone, as I just let it out.

"So, Nick and I have been talking. He's asked me out a few times, and I said no, because we had just got here, and I wasn't ready. He said he wasn't going to stop trying, and I had just admitted to myself today that I didn't want him to stop."

I pause, hoping the words will just come to me.

"Well, he found me just as the countdown started, and when it hit zero, he kissed me. I didn't pull away at first, and I kissed him back, but then, it was like I had a bucket of cold water thrown on me. I pulled back, found Royce, and he brought me here."

No one moves or speaks for such a long time that I finally take my eyes off of the fire and look around. By the time my eyes make their way to my dad, I'm crying, and I can't seem to stop. Mom hugs me a bit tighter, and Royce hugs me from the other side.

No one says a word until the tears stop. I expected yelling, or how could I have let this happen, but there isn't an ounce of anger. Even Jason, whose face was filled with rage the last time I saw it, is calm.

When I finally get a hold of my emotions again, my dad speaks softly.

"How do you feel about it?"

I don't know how to answer him, so I go with the truth.

"I'm not sure. That's what I've been trying to figure out. To be honest, I know I don't want to do the full courtship like Ella did, but I know I don't want to date like normal either. Is there an option in between?"

"We always knew you would do things your own way, once you figured out what that was. We'd like you to keep some high standards of modesty, of course, but we'll support you in whatever you choose to do. You're the one who has to live your life. We just want you to understand that there can be some heavy consequences as well. I know when you decide to do something that it's after a lot of thought. So, we just ask you to do that. Think about it, and we'll support you 100%." My dad says, leaning in to hug me.

"I'm on your side always, and I have your back. No matter when or where just call me, and I'll be there," Royce tells me.

"Same goes for us," Ella says.

Mom and Dad kiss me good night and head to bed, as Royce goes to his room, leaving Jason, Ella, and me in the living room.

"We talked to Nick, and he had no idea about the courtship. He was busy with the

BBQ contest and award aftermath when Ella and I were courting. He's really sorry, and he swears he will make it up to you," Jason says.

I nod, but I have no idea what to say to that.

"Do you want some sister time?" Ella asks.

Before I can answer, Jason says, "I can go sit in the truck and give you two some time."

"No, stay here. I'd like to go sit on the front porch and get some fresh air if that's okay?" I ask.

Ella and I put our jackets back on and grab a blanket, before heading outside. We settle down in the swing at the far end of the porch. It's my favorite place in the whole house to cuddle up and think or read.

We snuggle up together and get under the blankets to stay warm. Ella links her arm in mine and rests her head on my shoulder. She may be my younger sister, but she got married first, so she has a lot more experience in this department.

"What was your first kiss like?" I ask her.

She waited until her wedding day for her first kiss, even though, they didn't kiss at the ceremony. Jason pulled her away, and they had their first kiss alone. I think it was really romantic, but we never really talked about it until now.

Ella sighs, and when she talks, I can hear the smile in her voice.

"It was nothing like I thought it would be because I couldn't have imagined a more perfect moment. He was gentle and sweet, but he also used the right amount of hard and rough. There were sparks, too. Everyplace he touched me there were sparks. I felt that kiss for hours afterward. The feeling of his lips on mine never went away."

"That's how it felt, when Nick kissed me," I whisper, almost scared to admit it out loud.

Ella sits up and looks me in my eyes, searching for what I don't know.

"It's okay to enjoy the kiss, Maggie. I know Nick is a good guy, and I know he likes you, and he has for a while. I know you like him, and I see how you two are together."

"I did like the kiss."

"Then be honest, what made you pull away?"

"I got scared. His tongue touched mine, and I panicked."

Ella rests her head back on my shoulder again, and it's easier not having to look at her face.

"Do you regret waiting, until your wedding day?" I ask her.

"Not really, and I also don't think I'd have regretted it if we had kissed sooner. I knew he was it for me. He was the strong one, and I was the one always trying to push the boundaries when we were together."

"Ella!" I laugh.

"He wasn't going to do anything to go against Dad, so he followed Dad's rules to the letter. I really love that about him. That he respected me enough to do that."

"That's what I want. Someone willing to respect me no matter how crazy it is, because I'm not sure what my limits are, and I might not know until we push against them."

"The right guy will respect that, and I know Nick will. You just have to talk to him."

"Ella, how was..." I stop myself. I don't think I can ask her this. A girl's wedding night is between her and her husband, but I don't really trust anyone else enough to ask, and I'm dying to know what to expect my first time.

I won't admit that I read romance novels almost as fast as I can get them on my tablet. Some of the heroines are virgins, and it's mixed on if it hurts or not. I really want to know.

"You can ask me anything. I hope you know that," Ella says gently.

"I'm just wondering was your first time was like... Did it hurt?" I whisper. I'm not sure why, because no one is out here with us, but I'm still scared to ask.

"It hurt some, but Jason was amazing at distracting me. Again, I think it's all about the right guy, who loves you and cares about you enough. He will see to your comfort and pleasure more than his own."

We swing and watch the night sky in silence a bit more.

"Do you want to date him?" Ella asks.

"I like him, but I don't know what my version of dating looks like, and I don't know if that's fair to him, until I do," I speak the thoughts that were in my head earlier tonight.

"Maybe, tell that to him, and be open and honest. I really think he'll get it more than you think he will."

"Maybe. Will you be mad, if I bail on you tomorrow on taking down the decorations? I don't want to see him until I know what I'm going to say, but I promise, I'll talk to him this weekend."

"That's fine. Sage, Riley, and Sarah are going to help. Megan would like to, but Hunter wants her to rest since she has the weekend off from the shop." Ella says.

"How is your schooling going?" I take the chance to change the subject and give my mind a break. Ella is going to cosmetology school, and she graduates this summer. Megan owns the beauty shop in town and promised Ella a place when she graduates.

"Really well. Megan lets me come into the shop, and she teaches me as well. I answer phones and clean a few days a week to get to know the people there. Originally, I was going to take Anna Mae's place, but she told Megan last week she thinks she wants to stay. I graduate a month after Megan is due, and the school helps with testing, and if I pass, I should have my license not long after. So, Megan is going to stay home with the baby and just come in to do book work for a few months."

"What about after that?" I ask.

"Well, she has the chairs for us to each have our own. Jill, her assistant manager, can do ordering and all. So, Megan has been thinking of going part-time for a bit. It's a play by ear kind of thing. I don't have to work and neither does Megan, so we've talked about both doing it part-time, and then filling in for the other girls as needed, once I have built my client base."

"I never would have thought there were enough clients here to warrant four girls in the shop." I laugh.

"Well, the old ladies come in every week to get their hair and nails done and to get the local gossip. Then, add in we're the only hair place within a thirty-mile radius, so we get business from several towns over. Now that Anna Mae has won a few awards, we have had some ladies come down for the day, get their hair done by her, and then go get lunch at WJ's and do some shopping."

"Nick has done a lot for this town," I say more to myself than to her.

"He has, Maggie. Will you make me a promise?"

"Maybe."

"Will you leave your heart open, just a little? I know it's scary, but if you leave it open, then love has a chance to find you, and you deserve it more than anyone I know."

I hug Ella tight. "I promise Ella Bug. I promise."

Now, to figure out how to keep that promise.

Chapter 4

Nick

I'm heading into the bar for my meeting with Jason. I don't know what he wants to talk to me about, but all I can think about is Maggie. How did the conversation go last night? How much do her parents hate me? Does Maggie hate me?

I don't think I could deal with Maggie hating me, even if she has every right, too. In fact, she should hate me. She told me she wasn't ready to date. I knew it, yet, I pushed my way in and took her first kiss that was meant for her wedding day. For her *husband*.

Even in my head, I spit that word out. The thought of Maggie marrying anyone but me rips my heart out, and I don't think I can stomach it.

When I walk into Jason's office, he looks up, appearing about as tired as I feel. Doesn't seem like he got much sleep last night either. I close the door behind me and sit down.

"Did you talk to Maggie last night?" I ask first thing because I have to know.

"Yes, she sat us all down and told us what happened. She isn't mad just more like confused. She and Ella stayed up for a bit talking, so it was a long night."

"I still have no idea how to fix this, but I swear, I'm going to," I tell him.

"I'd start with her parents first and smooth things over. They'll always be on Maggie's side, but they might be able to help you if you let them." Jason says and then eyes me. "You look like shit."

"Thanks," I say sarcastically. "I didn't sleep much. Maggie was all I could think about."

"Well, let me give you something else to think about. Ella and I have been talking, and we want to make you a partner in WJ's."

"What does that mean?" I ask him.

"Well, we both agree you have more than done your share in making WJ's what it is today. Your cooking alone put it on the map. We've been friends for over a decade, and you have been here with me at WJ's almost as long. You don't feel like an employee anymore, and I think it's time to make it official."

My mind races, thinking about not only just being a chef but to own a stake in the place, too. Also, to be able to take that next step in my career. I start doing the calculations in my head. How much money can I put up to buy in?

"Stop it, Nick. I don't need an investor. You're a sweat equity partner because you've put in more than enough sweat. Ella and I want to start a family sooner rather than later, and she wants me home more. You have done a lot with bringing in more people. I want you to keep it up; go defend your title later this year in Dallas. Maybe, join a few more competitions and make a name for this place. Help me with openings and closings more, and bringing in new ideas."

My mind races. I can do this, and more importantly, I want this more than I realized. I don't even have to hesitate with my answer.

"Yes," I say, and Jason's face lights up.

"I expected you to tell me that you have to think about it, and you would give me your answer on Monday." Jason laughs.

"No need to think about it. Being partners, with my best friend in a business I love in a town I plan to make my home, is a no brainer."

"Perfect, then you can start by managing this Sweetheart's Dance coming up for Valentine's Day. I'd go talk to Jo at the diner and see what she has planned for the day, so we can coordinate."

The Sweetheart's Dance has been happening at the bar since the year it opened over sixty years ago and has become a town staple. Over the years, a legend has been rumored that who you attend your first Sweetheart's Dance with is your soul mate, who you will end up marrying.

Some just rack it up as a superstition, but I've seen it happen time and time again. My parents' generation has many couples to show from the Sweetheart's Dance. My parents for one, Hunter's parents, and Jason's parents.

Jo met her husband the day before the dance. They went together and have been together ever since. That's why she makes such a big deal of working with us every year. I respect the tradition and have yet to attend a dance myself. Although, I have worked several, but I've never been a guest.

I want to go with Maggie, but with this new partnership with Jason, it's best I don't open that door. I need to give my all to Jason and prove he made the right choice with me. It's for the best. We need to let the dust settle with all of this anyway.

I decide to walk over to the diner to talk to Jo. She has always done a Sweetheart's Breakfast the day of the dance and then stayed open for lunch later that day until the dance started.

She always makes her famous sweetheart cookies for the dance. They are heart cookies that aren't quite sugar cookies, but she won't share the recipe. It was her mother's recipe, and with any luck, she will pass it on to her daughter to carry on, because they are a huge hit every year.

I walk in, and Jo greets me with one of her big hugs, pulling me to the counter. She shoves food in my face, as we talk business, and she shovels more food in my mouth, as we talk about my parents, and how things are going at the bar. She helps customers in between, and before I know it, an hour has gone by.

When we have settled everything we need to, I say my goodbyes and turn to head back to the bar, when I see Maggie's parents, sitting at a table at the front of the diner. It seems like a sign that this is the time to talk to them, and I'm not one to ignore a sign.

I walk over to their table and take a deep breath.

"Mr. and Mrs. Stevenson, I was hoping I could have a word with you," I say.

Mr. Stevenson has no emotion on his face, as he looks me over. I expected him to be angry, and I deserve it. He looks over at his wife, who gives a slight nod, and then he turns back to me.

"Sure, have a seat," he says.

I take my time sitting down, trying to figure out what I'm going to say.

"I know Maggie told you what happened because Jason told me she did. I wanted to talk with you and apologize. I had no idea about the courtship, and how your family handles dating. I was so busy when Jason and Ella dated, and by the time things settled, they were married. Jason explained it to me last night, and I don't even know how to make this right, but I promise you, I will." I catch my breath and wait for one of them to speak.

"Maggie has always been very independent. We knew she would follow her own path, as her teenage years started. I'm surprised she held on to our beliefs this long. I think seeing Ella get married and take on a new role has shown her she needs to decide what her next step is." Mr. Stevenson pauses like he's waiting for me to say something, but I have no idea what.

"Maggie told us last night, yes," Mrs. Stevenson says. "She's trying to sort it out in her mind where to go from here. She's the only one who can decide what the future looks like for her, and what's right for her. The same way only you can decide that for yourself."

"So, we want to know where you stand." Mr. Stevenson takes a blunt approach.

I can still feel Maggie's lips on mine, and how right that moment felt. Then, the bar flashes through my mind. I have to prove to Jason I can be his partner, and I can't do that if I'm trying to win Maggie over, too. And if I screw things up with Maggie, then that could mess things up with Jason and me too, because he's protective of Maggie, because she's his family now.

"I've been asking Maggie out for a while now, and she puts me off every time. Then today, Jason offered me a partnership at WJ's. Not just to be an employee and chef, but a partner. I agreed, and I want to give that my all. My first task is this year's Sweetheart Dance. I really like Maggie and plan to make this right with her. By the grace of God, she might forgive me, and if that day comes, I'll gladly court her, if that's her wish. But I think it's best to let the dust settle right now, and then let her figure out what she wants." I speak the truth.

Neither of them speaks, as they mull over my words, and I see Jo giving me a sympathetic look. She knows what goes on in this diner and pays attention to conversations, even if she never speaks of them. So, I know she has heard this one, and I know she now knows what's going on. I also know she won't say a word about it to anyone. Jo is the one person immune to the Rock Springs' gossip tree.

"Maggie is independent and knows her mind. She doesn't make decisions lightly, and I know she'll think of nothing else but this today, and she won't stop until she figures it out. We'll support her no matter what she wants. If it's courtship, or even if it's dating your way. She's the one who has to live with her choices, and all we can do is guide her to making the right ones and support the ones she makes."

I mull over his words. This is not how I saw this conversation going. I pictured being yelled at and berated for making their last daughter impure. I even had a nightmare of a shotgun wedding, but to be honest, the wedding part wasn't the nightmare. It was the shotgun her father had pointed at my head. The thought of marrying Maggie doesn't scare me one bit.

I try to push that out of my head. I know it's right to let things settle down now and focus on this dance.

"I really am sorry about all this, and I hope there's a way I can make it up to you," I tell them.

They are both quiet a bit longer. Mr. Stevenson reminds me of my father, who says he likes to listen to people talk because you can learn so much. People seem to have a need to fill the silence he says, and they will lay more of their cards on the table than they realize. He taught me to value silence, so I'll wait Mr. Stevenson out.

"Just make Maggie happy, and we'll be fine," Mr. Stevenson says. "As a father, all I want is for my little girl to be happy."

"I will, and I promise to fix this," I tell him.

We say our goodbyes, and as I leave the diner, I decide to head the opposite way of WJ's and take a walk down Main Street. I don't have any destination in mind, but I think over the previous conversation. I still don't know how to make it right with Maggie.

I see the church, and like a beacon pulling me in, I see her truck in the deserted parking lot. Without thinking, I change course and head towards the church to talk to Maggie.

Chapter 5

Maggie

For years, the one place my mind always seems to quiet long enough for me to think has been in church. So, I made my way here this morning. Pastor Greg offered to talk to me, but I said I needed some time, so he has left me alone here in this old, country church to figure things out.

I love this church more than our old one in Tennessee. That one had gotten more commercial, bigger, with lots of fancy lights, and sound equipment. It lost that old feeling touch of a simpler time. This church here, in Rock Springs, still offers a small-town country feel. There's no fancy equipment just you, the church, and the preacher.

The walls have wood panels, but they have all been painted white and really brighten up the place. There are hardwood floors, and the large windows let in plenty of light. I love the amount of daylight in the church. It's not closed off and stuffy like so many I have seen while traveling with my dad.

I sit a few rows back from the front and stare ahead. While I watch the clouds roll by, I think of Nick. The kiss keeps rolling over and over in my head. If I'm honest with myself, after talking to my parents, I liked the kiss. I wouldn't mind doing it again. I try not to let lust control my thoughts.

I think of Nick. How do I feel about him? He's sweet and caring. He's also protective and reminds me of Royce in that way. Would I have liked that kiss, if it was from anyone else? I think of the Thorn boy, who wanted to court me back in Tennessee, and I instantly know I wouldn't have felt the same about the kiss if it had been him. *That kiss was amazing because it was Nick.*

What do I see in my future with Nick? Is there a future with us? If I'm honest, I hope so. I think it's fear more than anything that's holding me back, and I don't like to think I'm afraid.

I know I want to build my photography business, and it's the last thing I need to talk to my parents about. I should have done it last night, but it didn't even cross my mind. After what happened last night, I know without a doubt, they will support me.

I know they will support me when it comes to Nick too, and that's what gives me the courage to admit to myself what I really want.

Behind me, the sound of the door opening and closing again fills the air, but I don't hear footsteps. I don't turn around, I just assume it's Pastor Greg, and he will stop by and see how I'm doing.

I close my eyes and think of that kiss again. Nick's mouth on mine, his hand on my hip, his other hand in my hair, and I know then I have my answer if I'm not afraid to admit it to myself. The next time Nick asks me out, I'm going to say yes. I'm going to go on my first date, unchaperoned, and I want to end that date with another kiss.

I open my eyes and nearly jump out of my skin. Nick is sitting in the pew in front of me and has turned to face me. His eyes study me with concern.

"I didn't mean to scare you, but I didn't want to disturb you with your eyes closed either," he whispers. That makes me smile. I don't think Nick is a church guy, but the fact that he feels the impact of this place enough to whisper is all I need to know. It's how it makes me feel, too.

"It's okay. I heard the door, and I just thought it was Pastor Greg. Honestly, you were the last person I expected to see."

I have to be imagining the light pink that tints his cheeks. There's no way little old me could make a man blush. I have zero flirting game and wouldn't even know where to start.

"I saw your truck, and I wanted to talk to you, and then apologize about last night. I swear I didn't know about the courtship or any of it, Maggie."

"I know you didn't." I begin to talk, but he cuts me off.

"I still don't know how I'm going to make it up to you, but I swear it I will, Maggie. Tell me how to make this up to you..."

He won't stop talking, and I don't know what else to do, so without thinking, I lean forward and kiss him.

Just like last night, his lips are warm and soft, but he doesn't kiss me back. Thinking it's from the shock, I push him a little, and when he still doesn't move, I go to pull back, and that's when he springs to life.

He brings his hands up to frame my face, pulling me back into the kiss. He takes control, and I happily give it to him. This time when I gasp, his tongue finds mine, and I don't pull away. He leads me in this passionate dance that's doing all kinds of things to my nerves, and I let myself enjoy it.

He slowly pulls back just as out of breath as I am, and he searches my face like he's waiting for me to run again, but I'm not going anywhere. When he realizes that, he pulls me into him, resting his forehead against mine.

"I swear, Maggie, that was the last thing on my mind when I came in here. Now, it's all I'll be able to think about," he whispers.

"Me too," I tell him, before pulling back.

"What was on your mind, when you came in here?" I ask him.

"I was going to beg for your forgiveness, and then, say I was going to give you space and not bother you anymore, so you don't feel pressured."

"What if I don't want you to give me space?" I ask him.

His eyes roam my face before he shoots them skyward and closes them for a brief minute like he's sending up a silent prayer.

"I think we need to both take a step back, Maggie."

My heart sinks. Of course, that kiss meant more to me than it did to him. It wasn't his first kiss, and I'm being stupid to think it was the start of anything. I move to stand up, but he grabs my hand, pulling it to his mouth. He gives it a slow, warm kiss that freezes me in my place.

"Don't let your mind run wild. That kiss... I've never felt anything like it. I just don't want to pressure you into anything. Then, this morning Jason offered to make me partner at WJ's, and I think I need to prove to him that he made the right choice."

"Oh, Nick, that's wonderful." I soften. This is a huge thing for him, being a partner of the place. "You'll do amazing, and you've already done so much for the place. Jason knows he made the right choice."

"I hope so. He asked me to take over this year's Sweetheart's Dance, and I want to make sure I do it right. I don't want to promise you or him something, and then not be able to hold up my end."

He doesn't let go of my hand, so I just nod my head. This is for the best, right? He probably wouldn't be able to keep up with me, as I figure out this dating thing and still help with WJ's.

"I think it's the right thing to do. I don't know what I want dating wise just yet, and I know planning an event, like the Sweetheart's Dance, will keep you busy. Ella has been talking about it."

"Take this time and figure out what you want." He nods and stands. Then, he drops a kiss on the top of my head, before walking back out of the door.

I decide to stay and sit here a bit longer, so there's no chance of running into him when I finally head out to my truck.

I pass Pastor Greg on my way out, as I stop and thank him for opening the church to me. When I get in my truck, I take a large shaky breath.

What did I expect? Would he be waiting there for me after the way I reacted to that kiss? Who wants a girl who runs scared the second a guy kisses her? This isn't courting Maggie, this is the real world.

My thoughts are broken by my phone ringing. I notice it's Ella, so I turn it on speaker. I could use something else to concentrate on.

"Maggie!" Ella laughs. I love that she's so happy, since marrying Jason. I can only hope to find a guy that makes me as happy.

"Jason made Nick a partner!" She squeals.

"Yes, I heard." I try to sound happy for her.

"How did you hear?" She asks.

"I actually ran into Nick just now, and he shared the good news."

Ella is quiet for a moment, and when she speaks, her voice is soft.

"Did you two talk?"

"Yes, and I made it clear that I'm ready to date, and he made it clear that he isn't. He said that he needed to give his full attention to the partnership. So, thank Jason for me," I snap at her, and instantly, I regret it.

"I'm sorry, Ella. That isn't fair. I'm happy for you both, but the timing just sucks. Then stupid me, believed him when he said he wasn't giving up. He kisses me, I run, and he gave up pretty easy."

Ella's quiet again, and I just sigh.

"Why don't you help me plan this Sweetheart's Dance? I was going to ask you last night, but everything happened. I want us to spend some time together, and I want to do another photo booth, like at New Year's. We need to replace some of the decorations this year, and it could be fun a sister's shopping trip."

She sounds so hopeful, and I know that I can't tell her no. I know Nick said he was taking over the dance, but I can do shopping with Ella and some decorating. No big deal, right?

"Okay, let me know what you need."

"Great, we're lining up a few more people, but there's going to be a meeting at WJ's on Tuesday to go over everything. If you come, I promise to feed you."

Chapter 6

Nick

It's been three days, since my talk with Maggie, and three days, since that kiss. Three days, since I last touched her or kissed her, and I feel like I'm about to crawl out of my skin.

Despite my best efforts, she has been on my mind constantly. I worry I hurt her, and I worry she might find someone else. I also worry she's on a date with someone, and that someone else is getting those sweet, addicting kisses.

I try to push it all from my mind because the more I think of those kisses, the harder I become, and that's not a good thing when you're getting ready for a meeting. Today, I have the first meeting for the Sweetheart's Dance. This is to assign roles, get ideas going, and make a plan.

I know Ella has rounded up some of her sisters to help. With five sisters-in-laws, plus

Maggie and Lilly who are as close to a sister as you can get, there's no shortage of help.

I set up a few tables with water when Jason and Ella walk in. Then, my breath catches in my throat, when I see Maggie just behind them. She looks even more beautiful with her hair pulled back in a ponytail and no makeup on. Even hotter than she did all dressed up on New Year's.

My cock starts getting hard, so I tear my eyes away from her and sit down to get control over it before I embarrass myself.

When they get to the table, Maggie's eyes finally meet mine and hurt is written all over them. It looks like she hasn't been sleeping, and the thought that I could have caused that eats at me. I make a mental note to talk to her, after the meeting.

I try to tell myself the talk is just to make sure she's okay, but I'm not fooling myself. Talking to her would be for a very selfish reason. To be close to her, to maybe touch her again, and my body is hoping for another kiss. Though, I know I won't let it go that far, because it's not fair to her.

"Sarah plans to help with setup, but her friends Sky and Jenna, are visiting this weekend and haven't left yet, so she's spending time with them," Ella tells me.

Sky and Jenna are Sarah's best friends. They are the ones that finally got her and Mac together. They are also the ones with a cowboy fetish, so as much as she's telling me Sarah that will help later, it's warning me to keep my distance from the ranch for the time being. They will hang all over me, and that's the last thing I need Maggie to see right now.

"Okay, so it's just us?" I ask.

"Yes," Ella confirms.

We dive right in, and Jason pulls up pictures of the past year's dances and decorations. He and Ella agree to go through the decorations and make a list of what needs to be replaced.

"Maggie, you should set up a photo booth, like you did for New Year's," I tell her, finally making eye contact with her for the first time since we sat down.

"I said the same thing!" Ella adds, looking at Maggie. "Everyone seemed to like it, and you said you made some good money."

I loved the idea of having Maggie at the New Year's party when it was brought up. She setup and got to keep the money from the event, so I hope she agrees to do it again this time.

"I did, and I also got a newborn baby shoot out of it," Maggie says.

"Oh, are the photos from Lilly's wedding ready? Maybe, ask her if you can show them off at the dance. With all the connections that can be made at the dance, there are sure to be a few weddings in the future."

"What do you mean?" Maggie asks, looking around the table.

"You haven't heard the Sweetheart's Dance legend?" Jason asks with a big smile on his face.

"No." Maggie even looks beautiful, when she's confused.

"Legend says, that who you attend your first Sweetheart's Dance with and dance under the lover's ball is who you will marry," Jason tells her.

"Oh, that sounds like something made up to sell tickets to the lonely people." Maggie waves her hand at Jason.

"It's true. In my parents' generation, there were eight couples that came together here at the Sweetheart's Dance over a three year period. It's about time for our generation." I tell her.

"I don't believe that, but I'll be sure to keep it in mind when choosing my date." Maggie shakes her head.

My heart races at the thought of Maggie at the Sweetheart's Dance with another man. Yeah, that's not happening. No way. Not happening.

"You don't need to worry about a date. If you go with anyone, it will be with me, or you'll go alone," I say in a stern, no nonsense voice. Without even thinking, I laid all my cards out on the table, and I don't even care.

"And who did you go to your first dance with?" She gives me a smug look.

"No one. I've only worked in the kitchen for them. Unlike you, I do believe in the legend, and there wasn't anyone I wanted to take the plunge with until now." My eyes never stray from hers, as I speak.

Her perfect pink lips form a perfect O, as she looks up at me in surprise. The table is quiet; no one dares to say a word or even move.

"You're going to give a girl whiplash. Would you make up your damn mind?" She frowns, then turns to Ella, "What do you do for food during the dance?"

"Well, that's my department," I answer, causing her to scowl at me. She glares at me over the table and then sits up straight.

"Maybe, you should make those Parmesan Fries you made at Lilly and Mike's wedding. They went over good and would be easy to make."

I nod and make a note to add them to the menu. If Maggie wanted 24 karat gold French fries, I'd make it happen for her. That thought shakes me, as I finish my notes. It sounds like something my dad would say about my mom.

We talk a bit more about plans before Maggie stands up. "I'm going to go," she says.

"Oh, didn't you drive with Jason and Ella?" Since I know they have made plans to go through the decorations right now, they're not planning on leaving.

"No, I brought my own truck," she says.

"I'll walk you out." I follow her to the door, and then open it for her.

Just as she goes to open her truck door, I reach around her and hold it closed. She spins to look at me, and I pin her back to the truck with my arm still leaning on her door. Though I give her an escape route if she wants it, I'm thankful when she doesn't take it.

I decide to cut right to the chase and not play games with her anymore.

"I really meant what I said in the church. I need to concentrate on this Sweetheart's Dance and show Jason he made the right choice with me."

"Well, of course..." She starts in a sarcastic tone, and I know where her mind is. I hold two fingers to her mouth to silence her.

"Let me finish," I say, as gently as possible, waiting for her to agree. After a moment, she gives the slightest nod.

"But I haven't been able to stop thinking about you or craving you. The thought of you dating another man, or going to the dance with another man, is more than I can take."

"So, where does that leave us?" She whispers against my finger, which is still resting on her lips.

"I can't give you more, because I can't afford the distraction. Once things settle down, we can sit down and figure out dating any way you want. If you want to court, like Ella did, and not kiss me again, until our wedding day, I'll do it. I just can't commit right now."

Her eyes dart to the left, looking over my shoulder out towards the open field next to WJ's. I can see her mind turning, and I need to know what she's thinking. It's almost like she can hear me asking to read her thoughts, as her eyes snap back to mine.

"I'm not some puppy you can string along and expect to be waiting there for any scrap of attention. That's not fair." Her brown eyes go cold, as they narrow at me.

That statement hits me in the gut. It's not fair to her, but that's exactly what I was hoping for, wasn't it? That she'd be waiting for me when things settle back down.

"I know, and I won't ask that of you." It pains me to say it, but I know it would hurt her even more to agree to it.

"Then, we'll go our own ways and see where life leads us. If that's back to each other at the end of all this, then so be it."

Her words seem almost final, like a nail in my coffin. Will this beautiful, smart girl be there for me at the other end? I don't even notice I'm leaning towards her until the light blush crosses her cheeks.

Her tongue darts to her lips, and her eyes are laser focused on mine. I shouldn't do this, and I should give us a clean break, making it easier to start doing our own things. That's what I tell myself, but my heart is yelling, it's just one more kiss. One more kiss to tide you over. One more kiss to remind her we are meant to be together, and that even while we are apart, she's mine, and I plan to make good on it.

I lean in and use my hips to keep her pinned to the truck. I'm hard, and I know she has to feel it. I grind my hips against her, and when she gasps, I know she feels how much I want her. Her nipples are stiff peaks under her thin t-shirt, and she's as turned on as I am.

Knowing she's a virgin, untouched and innocent, makes these little moments even more of a turn on. Bringing my hand up to cup her cheek, I start to pull her in. The sound of gravel crunching under tires fills the air, but I don't care. There's nothing that's going to stop me from this kiss.

I inch closer slowly, making sure she can pull away at any moment. Her rapid breathing spurs me on. My lips barely ghost hers, when someone clears their throat, making Maggie gasp and turn her head away from me.

Damnit, whoever this is must have a death wish.

I pull back just enough to put an inch of space between us. When I look over my shoulder, I see the sheriff standing there, and I sigh.

"What can I help you with?" I ask him.

He eyes Maggie curiously, and I feel a need to shield her, so I shift, blocking Shane's gaze from her.

"I thought I'd stop here on the off-chance Sage was at the meeting today?" Shane says.

"No, she wasn't. Is everything okay?" I ask.

"No, we had another horse dropped off, but this time, it was taken right to Mike and Lilly's place. They just found it tied to one of the back fences. Not sure how long it has been there, but she was still drugged pretty heavy, so it couldn't have been long. I'm heading out that way now."

Maggie's hand grips the back of my shirt.

"I want to go to the horse and see if I can help them." She says softly behind me.

I turn to look at her over my shoulder, seeing the determination in her eyes.

"Okay, drive safe. I'm going to go let Jason and Ella know, and then, I'll be right behind you." I tell her.

I know I'm not needed, but knowing Maggie is there, I feel a need to protect her from anything that might go wrong.

"Okay, you can follow me over. This is the second horse in a few weeks, so the state police are also on their way there to see what they can find."

I nod, as he heads back to his car. Then, I turn to Maggie and open her truck door for her.

"Be safe, and I'll be right behind you. Stay out of the way, as there's no telling when that horse will come to, and it's so easy to get hurt when it does," I warn her.

She nods and buckles up. She turns her head, and our eyes meet. I hold her stare for a minute longer than necessary, before closing her door.

I watch her drive out of the parking lot and down Main Street behind the sheriff. I stand and watch her until I can't see her truck anymore, and then head in to tell Jason the news.

Chapter 7

Maggie

When I pull into Mike and Lilly's ranch, I take in all the cars already here. I recognize Hunter's truck and Sage's with the trailer on it. I'm guessing Mike and Lilly don't have a trailer yet, so she's there in case the horse needs to be taken to the clinic like Black Diamond did.

There are also two state trooper cars, the sheriff's car, and a few trucks I don't recognize. There's a flurry of activity down by the barn, but Megan catches my eye, as she sits on the front porch.

I make my way up and sit beside her.

"I was with Hunter when he got the call. He made me promise to stay up here and out of the way." Megan says as she rubs her tiny baby bump.

"Well, I second that. At least, until we know what's going on." I agree.

Nick's truck pulls in, and he parks beside mine.

"They're all so busy. Will you go down with Nick and see what's going on and let me know? I hate to bug Hunter, but the not knowing is driving me crazy." Megan smiles.

Nick leans against the front porch rail. "We can do that. Come on, Maggie. We'll find out some info, while still staying out of the way," Nick says.

I follow him down the steps and around the back of the house, as we walk down the drive to the barn.

We walk in a comfortable silence, neither of us willing to talk and break the spell. As we walk, I'm seeing the wedding Mike and Lilly had here just before New Year's. They didn't do anything big. It was just a simple wedding on their land, and Mike wanted to start the New Year with Lilly as his wife. I think it was the fastest wedding planned in town, at just one week.

They got married right in front of the barn with the snow on the ground from the freak snowstorm we had just before Christmas. They asked me to take pictures, and I couldn't have asked for a more beautiful setting.

As we near the barn, I slip back into reality, as Sage walks out and smiles at us.

"Megan sent us to get an update, because the not knowing, is killing her." I point my thumb over my shoulder towards the house.

"Well, this one is in as bad of shape as Black Diamond was, but it's even worse." Sage pauses.

"What do you mean?" Nick asks the question I can't seem to form.

"The horse is pregnant," Sage says, her face grimacing.

"How's... How's the baby?" I'm suddenly scared to ask.

"The heartbeat is faint, and Hunter thinks it's because of the drugs. It's impossible to know how far along she is. I was heading up to get my truck, so we can trailer her and take her to the clinic to do an ultrasound. Hunter wants to keep her there to watch, as the drugs wear off." Sage pauses, her voice breaking.

"He's not sure the foal will make it." She whispers, almost afraid to say it out loud.

"I want to see her," I whisper.

Nick looks hesitant, but we make our way into the barn, careful to stay out of the way. Everyone is gathering around a stall, and as I get my first glimpse of the horse, I gasp. She's as white as snow, and calm because of the sedative, but you can make out every bone in her body.

"Snow White," I whisper more to myself.

"I think you just named her," Lilly says, as she comes up beside me.

"I'm going to go help Sage get the trailer backed up," Nick says and heads out.

Lilly takes my arm and guides me out to the side of the barn.

"That's going to be her name, Snow White," Lilly says, as we lean against the gate.

"It suits her," I say.

"So listen, just a friendly heads up. I think Ella and Riley have it in their heads to play matchmaker with you and Nick," Lilly says.

"What do you mean?" I ask her.

"Well, Riley was all excited it worked pushing Mike and me together, so she has convinced Ella she can do the same for you and Nick. It's from a good place, because they just want you to be happy, but I figured I'd give you a little warning."

"Thanks," I mumble.

Lilly pats my shoulder, before walking back into the barn. Well, it's obvious this Sweetheart's Dance meeting was a setup then. I guess, we need a sister night, so I can tell her what Nick said, and then reassure her that her efforts will be in vain.

Sage backs her trailer up to the barn door, and as she gets out, she's stopped by a young state trooper, and they both glance over at me. As Nick walks up, he looks at me, and the muscles in his jaw flex, as he gives me a heated, almost angry look, and then walks into the barn.

The state trooper walks over to me, looking a bit hesitant.

"Maggie, right?" He asks.

"Yes." A bit nervous.

"Oh, Sage just told me your name. I heard you named the horse Snow White, and I wanted to come out and introduce myself. I agree it's the first name that came to my mind too when I saw her." He holds his hand out to shake mine. "I'm Miles."

"Nice to meet you, Miles." I shake his hand, taking him in. He's something to see in his tan and blue Texas state trooper uniform. He fills it out nicely. His muscles are as big as Nick's, but he's just a little taller. There's enough hair visible under his cowboy hat to see it's a sandy blonde. I like Nick's dark brown better.

Why am I comparing everything to Nick? I need to stop this. If I am ever going to move on, then I need to forget about Nick. He's too busy for me anyway.

"How long have you been a state trooper?" I ask him.

"About five years. I've been stationed in Haskell, but asked to be assigned to this case, so I'll be in the area, until we close it. Have you lived in Rock Springs long?"

"No, my sister married Jason, who owns WJ's and moved here. Then, my brother met someone here, so my parents and I decided we wanted to be close to family and made the move just before Thanksgiving."

"How do you know Lilly and Mike?" He asks.

"Ahhh, that's a bit complicated. Mike was the senior ranch hand on the ranch Jason's family owns, and Lilly is Riley's best friend. Riley is Blaze's wife, and Blaze is Jason's brother. Sage, who you were talking to, is Jason and Blaze's sister, so Mike and Lilly are family, whether they like it or not." I laugh.

Miles smiles with a far off look. "That's the kind of community I hope to find and settle down in one day. I grew up in Dallas, and there are so many people. I never knew my neighbors, and it's a rare sight to walk downtown and run into someone you know."

I know that feeling. I've been to Dallas, and it's just too big of a city. It's so impersonal, and I couldn't imagine living there or raising a child there. I know many people do it, but it's just not for me.

"Yeah, that's one of the things I love about being here, is that you can't go into town and not run into someone you know."

"Where did you live before here?" He asks.

"A small town in Tennessee called Mountain Gap. It's not quite as small, since there's a college there, but everyone still knew everyone for the most part."

He smiles then looks down at his phone. "I have to get back in there but... Umm, I was wondering if you would like to go to dinner with me later this week, maybe? I'd really like to keep talking, and maybe, you can show me around town, as small as it is?"

I think about what he said. He's asking me out on a date. I look him over. He's not bad looking, and I'm sure many girls would swoon over him, but he doesn't make me feel like Nick does, when I look at him.

I can feel Nick's eyes on me when he looks at me, and I don't get that feeling with Miles. But Miles is pretty easy to talk to, so maybe, he would make a good practice date. Dip my toes into the dating world, get that pesky first date over with, and maybe, figure out how I want to go about dating.

I should be fair to him and tell him from the start that I want to take things slow and put an end to any thoughts of a kiss, after the date. Kissing anyone but Nick makes my stomach turn, and I don't want to lead Miles on.

I open my mouth to speak, but I don't get the chance, because a strong hand pulls be backward, and then a solid wall of muscle is in front of me, blocking any view of Miles.

Even if I hadn't seen the shirt earlier today, I'd know who this is based on the scent alone. A woodsy scent with just a hint of Italian spices. *Nick*.

"She's not available." Nicks grits out to Miles, leaving no room for negotiations, but that doesn't stop me.

"Nick!" I pound a fist into his back.

He looks over his shoulder at me, "Not now, sweetheart. We'll talk in a minute." His voice is softer, but that does not stop me from fighting him.

He called me sweetheart. He's never called me that before. I've heard Jason call Ella that, and I always thought it was the sweetest thing. But when Nick says it, it's hot and sexy.

"I'm sorry, I didn't know," Miles says and pauses, then relents. "I didn't know." Footsteps, which I assume are Miles, walk back towards the barn.

Once the sounds of footsteps disappear, Nick turns around to face me. I'm almost scared to look up into his eyes. What will I see there? Anger? Hurt? I don't think I could take it.

He places a finger under my chin and gently lifts my head up to look at him.

"Look at me please," he says so softly, just above a whisper.

When my eyes meet his, I don't see anger or hurt. I see that same look he had right before he almost kissed me in the parking lot earlier today. His eyes are sparkling, and for some reason, this makes me angry.

I take a step back, putting some space between us. How dare he go on and on today about not having time for me and needing to prove himself to Jason, and then stop me, when another man wants to take me to dinner.

"What were you thinking?" I ask him, trying to keep my voice steady.

He takes off his hat, running his hand through his hair, while looking at the ground. He puts his hat back on, before looking back up at me.

"I don't know, Maggie. All I was thinking, when I heard him ask you out, was that you were mine."

"I'm not yours. You refuse to go on a date with me, even after we kissed. You have done nothing but push me away." I almost yell. I try to walk around him, but he stops me with an arm around my waist.

"Yes, I'm busy, but I'm not seeing anyone else, and I don't want you to either. I can't promise a weekly date, but if you will give me this, I swear I will make as much time for you as I can."

I shake my head. "I deserve more than to be waiting on someone's back burner for whenever they have time for me."

I start to walk away, and this time he lets me. I don't stop, until I'm back at the house. Megan is nowhere in sight, so I get in my truck and leave. I can't stay here and run into Nick again. I might say something I can't take back.

Chapter 8

Nick

Tonight, I'm tending the bar. I insisted, because I want to get to know all aspects of the business, if I'm going to be able to help Jason out. It's been a few days, since Maggie walked away from me at Mike and Lilly's place, and her words still float around my head.

I deserve more than to be waiting on someone's back burner for whenever they have time for me.

The worst part is she's absolutely right. She does deserve more than me being an asshole, because I was jealous. That's exactly what it amounted, too. I didn't have time to date her, but I sure as hell don't want anyone else to either, and that's not fair to her.

I've been racking my brain for the last few days, trying to find a way to make this work. If anything, it showed me I'm not willing to walk away from her.

I scan the crowd at the bar again. It's fairly busy being a Friday night, and the talk has been completely on the dance. It's all about who is taking who, or who is wearing what, and I've started zoning them out.

Just tonight, I watched two dance dates be setup with the help of a little liquid courage. Now, I'm cleaning the bar, while listening to Kelli flirt with Brice. Anyone with ears can tell she's trying to hint at a date. Brice is ignoring her hard, but she hasn't given up yet.

"Are you planning on asking anyone to the dance?" Kelli asks Brice.

"No, my parents are a product of the Sweetheart's Dance legend, so I take it seriously. I'll come and show my support... alone." Brice gives her a pointed look.

"Well, maybe we can meet, and you can spin me around the dance floor a few times." Kelli leans in a bit closer to him.

"I don't dance." He says, leaning back.

I know Brice isn't a huge fan of Kelli. Not many people around here are. Everyone likes Sage and Colt; they are pretty popular in town. Kelli was a huge part in what kept them apart for so many years. She spread so many lies between the two, and they both believed her, instead of talking to each other.

Sage is Jason's adopted sister, and when Colt's mother died, and he needed a place to stay, Jason's parents took him in, too. By that point, Sage and Colt were best friends, and I guess, things grew from there. So, I got a firsthand account of the whole relationship.

Brice dated Sage for a bit, when she and Colt weren't together. They parted as friends, and when Kelli made a huge scene in the diner right after Sage and Colt got back together, Brice was the one to swoop in and put an end to it. That fed the gossip mill for weeks around here.

Sadly, that wasn't the last of it. She tried to break Sage and Colt up one last time here at the bar by sitting on Colt's lap in front of Sage. Colt dumped her on her ass so fast that she fell right on her butt, and it was the only time any of us can remember him yelling at a woman. Kelli ran off crying, and everyone said she deserved it.

Thankfully, Sage and Colt were able to work it out, and I heard Sage got her revenge. Something about an early wake-up call service. Since then, Kelli has been labeled high maintenance, and no guy will go near her, even for a one-night stand.

I did see her leave with a trucker passing through last weekend, so I guess she has moved on to non-locals. I think if she hadn't signed a lease on her shop on Main Street, she would have packed up and left, after the whole Sage and Colt thing.

"I can teach you how to dance." Kelli purrs in a way that gives me shivers, and not the good kind. She runs her fingers up Brice's arm, and he pulls away.

"I didn't say that I don't know how, just that I don't. Please stop, Kelli. You're wasting your time with me." Brice grits out. I hand him another beer, as he nods at me, stands up, and walks away.

Kelli glares at me, like I'm the whole reason Brice walked off. I know it's worthless, but I figure I will give it a shot anyway.

"You are trying too hard, Kelli. People here have long memories, and if you want people's opinions of you to change, then you need to show them you have changed. Pushing Brice like that? It's the old Kelli crap." She glares at me but doesn't say a word, as I shrug and go serve people at the other end of the bar. Can't say I didn't try.

There are a group of guys at the other end of the bar, talking about the horse that was dropped off at Mike and Lilly's. They're speculating on why the horse was left there.

"It has to be because she was pregnant." The man with the long, gray beard says.

"Must be. Hunter isn't sure if the foal will make it. He has the horse at the clinic now." The man next to him says.

"I heard they named her Snow White, cause her coat is all white, not a single spot on it." Man one says.

This warms my heart, because I know it was Maggie who named her Snow White. Maggie who is now back on my mind, and I'm no closer to finding a solution to my problem.

Then, an idea hits me. We are planning this Sweetheart's Dance together, so might as well make the most of it.

I ask the other bar hand to cover for a moment, as I step into the office.

I call Maggie, and my heart stops when her sweet voice answers the phone.

"Hello, Nick." Her voice is soft, like she doesn't want to disturb someone else in the room.

"Maggie." I sigh. She actually picked up, and even said my name. I snap out of it and get straight to the point, before I lose her.

"I was hoping we could meet to go over some things for the dance. It's been big talk at the bar tonight, and I have a few ideas. I can come down to the ranch, if that's easier."

There are some muffled voices before she talks to me again.

"Ella said tomorrow for lunch would work. Jason, Sage, her, and I can be there."

"Perfect, I'll bring lunch."

"No, we'll cook. You're the guest here. See you tomorrow, Nick."

She hangs up without giving me a chance to answer. That's fine I'm going to see her tomorrow, and it's enough of a reason to not wipe the smile from my face.

• • • ● • ● • ● • •

I pull into the ranch, driving past the barn to where Maggie and her parents are staying. She texted me first thing this morning, saying that everyone was going to meet there, and her mom insisted on cooking lunch.

The white farmhouse comes into view with its large front porch. I park in front and knock on the door. Maggie's dad answers the door and looks me over, before stepping aside and letting me in.

Everyone is already in the living room, so I take a seat in the free chair.

"We'll let you talk. Lunch will be ready in about half an hour." Maggie's mom says as she pulls Mr. Stevenson from the room.

Ella, who is curled up on Jason's lap, is laughing, as I look over at Maggie, who's at the other end of the couch, and my heart skips a beat.

We launch into talk of a few ideas I'd heard bantered around.

"I want to do a silent auction to help raise funds for the church. They would help cover the cost of these horses that keep showing up." I suggest. "I talked to Ella about it yesterday."

Everyone agrees they like the idea.

"I was thinking of bids for fun date ideas around town. Dinner for two at WJ's, and maybe, another dinner at the diner. Mike and Lilly offered up an afternoon of horseback riding and a picnic down by the lake on their place." Ella adds in.

"We could do a weekend getaway at the lake house, if Mom and Dad agree," Sage adds.

"Oh, that one will draw big money. We should post some photos of the house to really sell it. Then, we should ask around town, if anyone has any other ideas. Maybe, a weekend at the B&B, or some shopping credits at the stores downtown," Maggie says.

"What if we find some people offering to babysit, so a couple can go do their own thing, too?" Ella adds.

"I could prepare a packed picnic meal with some wine. Complete with a basket and blanket for them to take to their favorite spot," I suggest.

Maggie smiles over at me, and I make a mental note to take her on a picnic date, as soon as the weather warms up.

"Oh, since it's for the church, maybe, Pastor Greg will donate a few tickets to the Summer Carnival with an armband for rides. Everyone goes to that." Sage throws in.

Maggie adds to the list she has been keeping.

"Lunch time." Maggie's mom sings from the kitchen.

We all pile into the kitchen and grab plates. I'm surprised we all fit around their dining room table, but we do. I think Ella has a few tricks up her sleeve because somehow, I end up sitting next to Maggie. My thigh is pressed against hers, and our arms keep bumping into each other with how tight a squeeze it is at the table. I'm painfully aware of how close she is to me, along with her every move. It makes it very hard to concentrate on much else.

Maggie's parents ask questions about the dance, since this is the first one they will attend. Sage tells them about the Sweetheart's Dance legend, and the couples that have ended up married from it.

Once we are done eating, we wrap up the meeting, but Ella stops anyone from leaving. She starts searching through her purse.

"Oh, here it is. Maggie and I were supposed to go on Monday into Dallas to get what decorations we need, but I can't go. I just found out we have testing the next day at school, so I'm getting with a few of the girls to do some studying. Nick, will you go with Maggie?" Ella looks at me so innocently.

She isn't innocent. She's playing matchmaker. I know it in my gut, but honestly, I couldn't be happier for another excuse to spend a whole day with Maggie.

I look over at Maggie who is looking at me. She shrugs, and I smile.

"Of course. Where were you planning to go for decorations?" I ask her.

Ella hands me several pieces of paper all stapled together. "It's all on the list. I've been doing some research online. Oh, and if you value your life, you'll confirm the rumor of the bakery having heart peppermint bark for Valentine's Day. Apparently, they'll be selling it all year long now in some form or another."

I laugh, "I promise not to leave Dallas without it." Then, I turn to Maggie. "I'll pick you up at nine a.m. No point in trying to battle rush hour traffic."

Chapter 9

Maggie

I didn't think this through. Over an hour car ride into Dallas in the car with Nick. Every one of my nerves is well aware he's in the seat next to me. He's right there, and I can't touch him, and he won't touch me, after my little rant outside of the barn at Mike and Lilly's.

It's fine, I keep telling myself. I don't want him to touch me, and he's leaving me alone. Maybe, I should try to get a hold of Miles and at least apologize. He seemed like a really nice guy, and with Nick knowing where I stand, maybe it's not too late to accept that date.

Who am I kidding? I probably have drama stamped all over me; he'd do best to run the other way when he sees me coming. I can't blame him either. I sigh and look out of the window.

"Everything okay?" Nick asks.

"Yeah, just a lot on my mind," I answer honestly.

"Well, I'm a good sounding board, if you want to talk it out."

"Pass."

That one word ends the conversation until we get closer to Dallas, and I help navigate to the first store on Ella's list.

"What are we getting here?" He asks, grabbing a cart, as we walk inside.

"Mostly, balloons and napkins. They're having a helium pump delivered, so you guys can blow the balloons up, before the dance."

We find the balloons easy enough. Lots of red, pink, white, and silver, and they are heart shapes, mostly.

The second shop is in the same shopping center, thankfully. We pick up an order Ella placed online for some folding tables for the silent auction. Thankfully, Nick has a large truck.

At the next store, we get the centerpieces on our list, but we pass an entire aisle of photo props.

"Oh, can we go down here? I want to see what props they have."

"Of course." Nick follows me down the aisle, and I grab some decorations. Lots of hearts and love signs, along with some cute face masks for silly photos, and then some craft items to make a backdrop.

On the way back out to the truck, Nick turns to me. "You're really passionate about photography. Your face lit up back there just shopping for items for your photo booth."

I know I blush a bit at his heated gaze. "I really enjoy it. The way you can manipulate a photo by just changing your angle or changing up the lighting."

He studies my face, as he thinks about what I said, and I turn away from his gaze.

"Do you want to grab lunch? One of the contestants from the BBQ contest I was in, has a place not too far from here, and then, we can finish up the list."

That sounds a lot like a date. No, Maggie, not a date. It's just lunch because your sister forced you two to spend the day together when she bailed. I fully believe she made up some test to throw Nick and me together. I wouldn't put it past her.

Still, this feels very much like a date. Maybe, I should put him off, just grab some quick fast food, and keep going. But then, my stomach rumbles, giving away how hungry I am.

"Lunch it is," I sigh.

The smile that lights up his face is one that should come with a warning label. *Will send tingles to all your girl parts.*

We walk into a very modern and city feeling BBQ place. There's none of the rustic wood, like at WJ's. The place is all sleek with black and white tables and chairs and red accents.

We are shown to a table by a waitress, who is flirting just a little too much. Once we sit down, my immature side comes out, before I can pull it back in.

"Does that happen everywhere you go?" I ask Nick.

"What do you mean?" He sets his menu down and looks at me with a puzzled look on his face.

"Girls falling all over themselves to flirt with you."

"Who?" He asks, looking around.

Did he really not notice, or is he just being polite? Because I don't know how you could not notice the poor girl.

"The hostess," I say, watching him.

He shakes his head. "I didn't notice."

He's serious. He didn't notice her?

"How could you not?"

"You won't like my answer, Maggie."

Well, now he's got my attention.

"Try me."

"I didn't notice the hostess, or any other girl in here, since we walked through the door, because I was too busy, staring at your ass in those jeans."

Well, shit. I never thought I'd hold a guy's attention like that. It's a feeling that pushes my confidence to the front and gives me the power to do something that I normally wouldn't.

Old, non-dating Maggie would have blushed and changed the subject, or maybe, excused herself to the bathroom to splash cold water on her face. That Maggie was shy and still trying to figure out what she wanted.

This Maggie though, she smiles at Nick and says, "Good."

Shock covers his face before a blinding smile takes it over. I glance down at my menu, as the waiter comes over and takes our drink order. He winks at me, before walking away, and I guess now the tables are turned.

I look at Nick, who is watching me, and I wink at him, and he seems to relax. Nick starts talking about the menu and the dishes, which type of BBQ is offered, and what a great idea a few of the items are.

I watch him the whole time, because Nick in his element, is something to behold. His face lights up, and his passion shines through.

After we order, we talk a bit about what we have left to pick up for the dance, which is basically fabric and lights. Ella is doing some canopy thing with lighting she found online.

Nick talks about the BBQ competition he won last year, and how intense it was. You can tell by the smile on his face how much he loved it, though. Once the food arrives, we sample everything off of each other's plates, and the mood is so relaxed that we almost miss the woman who walks up to the table.

"Well, I'll be! One of my staff said they saw you here, Nick, but I didn't believe it. I mean, there's no way the winner of the BBQ Championship is eating lunch at the third-place winner's restaurant, so I had to come out and see for myself." The girl is way too bubbly, as she leans down to give Nick a half hug.

I don't know why, but I don't like her. Something about the way she looks at Nick like he's a piece of meat, and not the amazing guy that he is. It's a lot like how the hostess was looking at him. The one he says he didn't notice but trust me, he notices this girl.

"Maggie, this is Lauren. She was in the competition with me. I told you about her."

No, you told me about a person, not a girl, I think. But I plaster on a big smile and shake her hand.

"Of course, it's nice to meet you. Great place you have here." I try to use the manners my parents drilled into me growing up.

They start talking food, while I dig into mine, only half listening, until something she says catches my attention.

"You still working at that bar?" She asks Nick, but it's the way she said *bar* that got my hackles up.

"Actually, because of him winning the competition, and the TV special they did on Nick, the place doubled in business, and it's much more than a bar now. They have live entertainment and a lot of sit-down dining. It's actually bigger than this place." I look around the restaurant. WJ's really is bigger, if you include the outdoor dining space.

I look back at Lauren and smile, and boy if looks could kill, I know I struck a chord with her. I look at Nick whose eyes are shining at me with a huge smile on his face.

"Oh, and Jason just made him partner, so he's now an owner." It just keeps slipping out of my mouth, wanting to prove to her that he's better than her and her condescending tone. He is better, and the judges proved it with his first-place win to her third-place.

Nick's smile gets even bigger, and he reaches across the table, taking my hand in his. I should pull it away, but I can't. He's making a claim in front of this girl, and this simple touch from him calms me down. When he starts rubbing his thumb along mine, I lose my will to keep arguing with her.

"It's true, and it just happened last week. My first task is putting on the town's annual Sweetheart's Dance, which is why we are in Dallas, picking up decorations and supplies. I realized we were nearby, so I thought I'd bring Maggie to lunch." Nick's eyes never leave mine, and his smile never leaves his face.

"Oh, so you're here on a supply run. Got it." She says. She just made it very clear this isn't a date.

I know this isn't a date, but it feels like a date. Nick's been flirting with me like it's a date. He's holding my hand like it's a date.

Like he can read my mind, he squeezes my hand, "A supply run, and a good reason for a lunch date in the city."

Lauren frowns for just a fraction of a second. If you blinked, you would have missed it. Then, she smiles a fake smile, if I ever saw one.

"Well, enjoy your lunch. I need to get back to the kitchen. Nice talking to you." She says, and I swear I can hear her mental *not*, added to the end of her sentence.

On the way out after lunch, I smile over at him.

"What?" He asks.

"Lunch date, huh?"

He chuckles, "Yes, I asked, and you accepted."

"I accepted lunch, but I didn't realize it was a date," I joke.

"Well, it became a date, when you got jealous over the hostess and made me admit to paying more attention to your ass."

I clear my throat, trying to regain my composure because I'm sure I just swooned a bit.

"Don't dates usually end with a kiss?"

He looks at me with heat in his eyes this time, and before I can say a word, he has me pinned to the side of his truck. He captures my face between his hands, and then his lips are on mine. This kiss isn't slow and soft, like the ones before. This one is hard and passionate like he's claiming me.

I grab a hold of his shirt, pulling him closer to me, and he deepens the kiss. His entire body is pressed to mine, pinning me to the truck, and I've never felt safer, or more turned on in my life. The sensations are almost too much, and a second before I have to pull away, he does.

We both gasp for breath, as he rests his forehead on mine. Neither of us says a word for a moment.

"Does it qualify as a date now, sweetheart?" Nick whispers.

"Yes," I whisper back.

He leans down and gives me one more chaste kiss, before pulling back and helping me into the truck.

The rest of the day we have fun together. We get the last of Ella's shopping list and walk to some nearby stores hand in hand, before heading to the bakery and getting the red and white heart shaped peppermint bark.

Nick holds my hand the whole way home, as we talk about our childhoods. He tells me what it was like to grow up in Rock Springs, and I talk about Tennessee, and our day trips to Nashville, my parents work with the church, and what happened last fall with Ella and Seth. It ended with Seth trying to crash Ella and Jason's wedding, and in the end, it caused my parents to move to Rock Springs.

Chapter 10

Nick

What is that saying? All bad disasters start with good intentions. Well, that's how tonight started out. I was at the bar yesterday, and I overheard Ella and Jason talking about Blaze and Riley turning down a night out with Jason's family, because they couldn't get a babysitter so late.

They are the only couple with a kid. Baby Lilly is just over a month old. She eats, sleeps, poops, and loves to cuddle. How hard could it be, right?

So, I offered to babysit. I have experience, and they deserve a night out, as a family. Megan will have her baby this summer, and I'm sure there will be more pregnancy announcements to come, so who knows how many more nights out like this they might have. Besides, I love cuddling babies, so again, no problem, right?

Wrong. There's a big problem. Everyone left about an hour ago. I'm at the ranch house, because all the baby's stuff is here, and little Lilly hasn't stopped crying. She drank an entire bottle, I changed her, she burped three times, but I can't get her to calm down. I tried playing peek-a-boo, reading to her, rocking her, and even some white noise.

At this point, I think she's just doing it to see how far she can test me, but her little lungs sure are getting a good workout. I refuse to ruin this date night for the family, because I know Tim and Helen went with them.

Then, Maggie's face flashes in my mind, as I grab my phone and call her, getting ready to beg and bribe, if I have, too.

"Nick? What is going... Is that a baby?"

"Yes! I agreed to watch baby Lilly, and she won't stop crying. I don't want to ruin the family's night out. Can you help? I'm at the ranch house." I say breathlessly.

"Yes, I'm just at the house. Be there in a minute."

We hang up, and I don't worry about Maggie being able to find me. This house may be big, but Lilly is screaming so loud that I'm sure she will hear her outside. Only a few minutes go by, before Maggie calls out and follows the screams into the living room.

When Maggie finds me, I'm standing in the middle of the living room, shhing the baby and bouncing her, as her crying has only slowed down a fraction of a bit. I turn in a circle and find Maggie, leaning up against the wall watching me. Pure relief washes over me now that she's here.

Maggie has a small smile on her face, as she shakes her head and reaches for the baby.

"You're giving Uncle Nick a complex crying like this." She says and pulls a pacifier from out of nowhere, and the baby latches on and quiets down.

"How long ago did she eat?" Maggie whispers.

"I'm not sure maybe an hour ago."

"With all the crying, she might need another bottle."

When the baby spits out the pacifier and gets the look, like she's about to scream the house down again, I run to grab another bottle.

"There's only one more bottle. Riley only left three." Riley is breastfeeding, so I know she pumped just enough to have a little extra for tonight.

"There's more in the freezer, and I know what to do," Maggie whispers.

Lilly won't take the bottle and starts screaming again, so she sighs. "Come on. There's a little trick I learned running the nursery at church."

I follow Maggie, who wraps Lilly in a thick blanket from the couch and heads outside to the front porch. As soon as the cool air hits baby Lilly's face, she calms and takes the bottle. Maggie makes her way to the swing, so I duck in and grab another blanket, before joining them.

"You're really good with her," I say.

"Well, I worked the nursery for almost ten years at the church back in Tennessee. I love kids, and it taught me a lot of tricks. I did some babysitting too for families at church. If she has been crying for a while, she was picking up on your stress. Once she calms down, and you do, then things will be fine, you'll see."

Maggie stops to burp the baby, and then turns to me. "Want to finish feeding her?"

I nod and take a deep breath. Lilly snuggles right up against my chest and takes the bottle from me. Her eyes are wide and fixed on my face.

"Hey there, beautiful. We got off on the wrong foot, but I promise, I'll always be here for you. We'll learn this baby thing together. I also promise to be here to scare off every boy who thinks they're interested in you. Though, you have five other uncles, plus your dad, to help there, too. I'm so sorry your dating life is going to suck."

Maggie reaches over, and Lilly latches on to her finger. "It's okay, Auntie Lilly, Maggie, and Ella will be here to cover for you, and sneak you out of the house as needed. You'll meet some handsome cowboy who can cook and will sweep you off your feet. Maybe, you'll meet him, when you're young and grow up together, like Uncle Colt and Aunt Sage."

Maggie rests her head on my shoulder, as she keeps talking to baby Lilly, while she finishes her bottle. The baby has a grip on Maggie's finger but still keeps her gaze on me.

Something about this moment hits me in the gut. *This is the future I want.* Maggie and I ending a long day together on the porch swing cuddled up with our kids. No matter how much I fight it when I see my future, now Maggie is always in it.

I can't keep putting her off, because of WJ's, and expect this to work. I have to find a way to balance both, if this vision is to come true. If it's to be us, holding our own child on our own front porch, like this in a few years.

I burp the baby, and we get her to sleep. She cuddles up on my chest, and when baby Lilly sighs and with Maggie cuddled up to my side, all is right in my world.

"I want many nights like this with you and with our kids," I whisper, hoping the universe will hear it, and then make it happen.

Maggie doesn't say anything at first, and I have to wonder if she heard me, but then, there's the faintest whisper. "Me too."

We rock in the swing for a bit longer, before taking Lilly inside and laying her down to sleep. She doesn't even stir, as I lay her down. Poor thing tired herself out with all that screaming.

I pull Maggie down onto the couch with me, and she snuggles right up to me.

"Thank you for coming tonight. You're a natural with this. I never would have thought to take her outside." I say, kissing the top of her head.

"A mom of eight taught me that trick. It only works, when the air is cool. It's just something about the cold air. Works with their lungs, too. It cools them off and helps them to relax. Got to make sure they're bundled up to stay warm, though."

She turns to look up at me and smiles. I lean in and kiss her, just a soft quick kiss. I know immediately that this is it. I'd be an idiot to keep fighting my attraction to her.

"I'm going to make this work, Maggie. I promise you if you'll just be patient with me."

"Okay," she whispers, and then pulls me in for a deeper kiss. A kiss both needy and claiming.

This kiss is my promise to her that I'm going to make this work; I'm going to make her a priority. Her hands tangle in my hair, as she leans up and straddles my lap.

She's in thin black leggings and a loose gray sweater over a white t-shirt. I have on a pair of sweatpants and a t-shirt. I figure being relaxed, while babysitting was a good thing, but I can feel the heat from her pussy right against my now hard cock, and I'm wishing I wore jeans.

I want to pin her down and make her cum, watch her let go, and give herself to me, but I know she isn't ready for that.

When her hips grind against mine, I groan and grab her hips to stop her from moving again. Does she even know what she's doing?

"Maggie," I whisper against her lips. She tries to grind on me again, but I hold her still. "Sweetheart, this is a line I don't think you're ready to cross. I haven't even taken you on a proper date."

She kisses me again, before pulling away. "I've never been this turned on in my life." She mumbles against my ear.

"I know. Me either. I don't want you don't get me wrong, but I want to take you on a proper date, before we cross this line. Nothing more than kissing, okay?"

She sighs but nods. Moving her off my lap is one of the hardest things I've ever had to do. My cock screams at me, demanding to know what I'm doing, or if I've lost my mind.

Once she's sitting down beside me, I pull her in for another kiss. I'm addicted to the hint of cherry on her pink lips, and the way her lips mold to mine. Before I can deepen the kiss, she pulls away.

"I think it's best if I head home. Let you claim the glory for tonight, when everyone gets home."

"I'm going to plan the first date you deserve. One that pulls out all the stops, and I'm going to do it soon. You can count on that." I tell her.

She walks to the door, turns back, and smiles. "I don't doubt it, and I can't wait to see what you come up with. Just remember, I'm a simple girl, and I don't need anything flashy."

"Good to know."

She smiles at me again, before turning and walking out of the door. Maggie is anything but simple. She's sweet and soft, but she also has a bite to her when needed. She's strong willed and will give me a run for my money any day. She's still trying to figure herself out, and I want to help her figure out where she wants to be, and what she wants to do. I don't ever want to hold her back.

This is why I want to plan a date at my place. I want to show her around, because it's important that she likes my home. It's where I hope we will raise a family. I want to show her the animals and have her in my space, so when she leaves, her scent is there.

An idea begins forming in my head, and I know I need to get a few things in order, and set a time, where Jason is closing. I will talk to him tomorrow, pick a date, and then, make it happen.

No more waiting. *Maggie Stevenson will be mine.* She will be my first and only Sweetheart's Dance date. I send up a silent prayer the legend is true, because I need all the help I can get.

Chapter 11

Maggie

Today, I'm visiting Megan at the beauty shop to get my hair cut. That and to have a little girl talk. Afterward, we are going to have lunch together. I'm also going to be doing some spy work for my brother on Anna Mae.

I walk in, and the smell of nail polish, hair dye, and cleanser assault my nose. How Megan works in this day in and day out I will never know, but she loves it.

"Maggie!" Megan comes rushing over and gives me a huge hug. It's just what I need. Her hugs always put me in a better mood.

A few of the ladies in the shop all turn and smile at me. I don't remember their names, as it was all a blur the last time I was here. Megan drags me over to her chair.

"So, what are you thinking? Maybe, a short bob?" Megan asks.

"Oh no, dear! Don't cut that long hair, it's so beautiful. It reminds me of Carrie

Underwood." The little old lady with curlers in her hair says.

"Yeah, I don't want to cut it, but just a trim, and maybe, a new shape," I say.

"Is there someone you are trying to impress? Maybe, that hot chef over at WJ's?" The lady in Anna Mae's chair says.

"Grandma!" Anna Mae shrieks.

Ahhh, that is Mrs. Willow then. I've heard many stories about her.

"Maybe," I smile and blush just a bit. There really are no secrets in small towns. Many might hate that, but I find I love it.

"Well then, maybe we should style it too, and you can stop by Nick's to check on things for the Sweetheart's Dance, after our lunch."

The entire shop agrees and starts talking about when they met their husbands or significant others, and I don't remember the last time I laughed so much.

"I met my husband at the gas station." Mrs. Willow says. "My daddy let me borrow his car to go out with some friends and asked me to fill it up. I was pumping gas when he pulled in across from me. We talked while we filled the cars, and then I got in the car to leave. I was about to pull out of the lot when he ran up after me and ask me out. I ditched my friends that night, and we went on a date right then and there."

"I met my husband because he was my neighbor." The lady with the curlers says. "I had a dog who loved to play outside, and he kept accusing him of pooping in his yard and me not cleaning it up. Well, I knew it wasn't him, so we fought about it for weeks. Then one morning, we were both outside on our porches, my dog was inside, and this stray dog that had been hanging around the clinic comes and takes a shit in his yard, looks at him, and I swear that dog stuck his nose in the air and walked off! I had to run inside because I was laughing so hard. That day a dozen roses were delivered, and he asked to take me to dinner to apologize. I said it better be a steakhouse in Dallas, and he agreed. Been together ever since."

By the time we are done, my stomach hurts from laughing so much. My hair looks amazing with some beach waves and a great new style to it. Megan and I decide to walk down to the diner for lunch.

"I can see why everyone likes having a weekly appointment at your salon. It's like getting together with your best friends," I say.

"Yeah, it's why I love working there. I thought of taking some time off after the baby is born, but I'd miss it too much. So, I'm going to go down to part time. We'll see how it works out."

We walk in, and everyone smiles and waves.

"Hey, Jo!" Megan hugs her before we settle in our seats.

"Oh, Maggie, I'm so glad you're here!" Jo says. "I was thinking of redoing my menu and wanted to see if I could bring you in to photograph some food. I'd also like photos to use on my website and social media."

"Of course, I'd love to! You have my number, so let me know when works for you."

Jo nods and walks off to put our food in. I look around and notice Miles, sitting at the counter.

"There's Miles," I nod at him.

Megan looks him over. "He is pretty easy to look at."

"I feel like I owe him an apology for how Nick acted."

"Then go talk to him. I'll be here expecting the full details when you're done." Megan smiles.

I steady myself, walk over to the counter, and then sit down next to Miles.

"Maggie." He asks, a bit hesitant. Can't blame the guy.

"I think I owe you an apology." I start, and he holds up his hand.

"No apology needed. I was given the wrong information and didn't know."

"No, you weren't given the wrong information. Nick and I weren't together then. We'd tried, and he kept pushing me away, but

I think him seeing someone else was interested finally broke him."

Miles looks to the back wall and wraps his hands around his coffee cup, before looking back at me. "You two together now?"

"Yeah, we're taking it slowly."

He nods, "Good. I can tell you're happy because you smile when you talk about him."

I shake my head. "For what it's worth before he stepped in, I was going to say yes."

"Well, that counts for something." He gives me a small smile.

"I just felt like I owed you an explanation. I didn't like how we left things."

"Well, I hope we can be friends, Maggie. I don't know how long I'm in town for, and I could use a friend. People see the uniform and tend to shy away and give me my space."

"I'd like that. I hope you catch the guys doing this to the horses soon. Not because I want to get rid of you, but because I'd hate to see more horses show up."

"You and me both."

I head back to the table, and Megan smiles. "I love this seat. I heard it all." She giggles.

"You little spy!" We laugh and talk over lunch. Megan shares her pregnancy updates, and details about a conference Anna Mae is going to in Dallas. I tell her about our lunch in Dallas, and Megan laughs.

As we are wrapping up our lunch, someone stops by the table, and when I look up, Lauren is standing there. What in the hell is she doing here?

"Maggie, right?" She asks, and I just roll my eyes.

"This is Megan, Jason's sister," I say. "Megan, this is Lauren."

"Huh, you looked prettier on TV," Megan says, and I bite back a smile, as I watch Lauren's eyes go cold.

"What are you in town for?" I ask though I'm sure I already know the answer.

"Well, I thought I'd come and see Nick's place now that he's part owner." She says.

"Oh, too bad it's closed today," Megan says, but it's obvious she doesn't think it's too bad.

"I noticed. You don't happen to know where I can find Nick, do you?" She asks.

I do, but there's no way in hell I'd tell her.

"Nope," I say with a smile.

"Funny, no one here does," Lauren says.

"Well, the thing is this isn't Dallas. We're a small town, and we protect our own. No one knows you, so no one trusts you. No one will tell you anything." Megan says with a smile on her face.

I notice the diner is very quiet and pretty much everyone is staring at us. Many of them are even turned in their chairs to get a good view, while Miles is standing up from his stool, ready to jump in if needed.

"I noticed. So, I got a room at a B&B, so I can stop in to see him tomorrow for dinner." She says with saccharine sweetness and then walks out of the door.

No one in the building moves, so Megan breaks the tension. "Want me to claw her eyes out?" I laugh, and everyone slowly starts to get back to what they were doing before. I nod a thanks towards Miles to let him know I saw him. He touches his finger to his hat, before heading out of the door.

"No, but I reserve the right to change my mind," I tell Megan.

"Always."

· · · · · ● · ● · · ·

Tonight, Ella and Jason are having dinner with Royce, Mom, Dad, and me at our place. They do this a few times a month, and a lot of times, we will head to the main house and have dinner with the whole family. I really love living here, because there's always someone around to talk to.

Like tonight. After dinner, I pull Ella aside.

"Will you and Jason take a walk with me?" I ask her.

"Of course. Let me grab him and my coat."

We walk down a path away from the main house. It's a path I like to walk on a lot lately. It goes past Sage's family graveyard and ends at a small cabin that needs to be fixed up.

Ella is walking between us with one arm looped through my arm, and the other looped through Jason's arm.

"Everything okay?" She asks.

"Yeah, I think so, but I just have this feeling I can't shake, since lunch today," I say.

"What happened at lunch?" Ella asks.

"I'm shocked you don't know," I laugh.

"Well, I had school and came straight to dinner, so no chance to talk to anyone. You hear anything?" She asks Jason.

"No, I did inventory at the bar, and then came here to help Blaze with a few repairs on the barn."

I nod and recap lunch from talking to Miles to my run in with Lauren.

"I don't know. There was something in her voice and her look that has my gut screaming," I say.

"And who is this girl exactly?" Jason asks.

So, I tell him about the lunch Nick and I had in Dallas and don't leave out any details.

"And now she's here?" Jason asks.

"Yep, and maybe, I'm jealous, but I just feel like it's to cause trouble," I tell them.

"Maggie's gut is always right. She knew Jenna Masters was not being an honest friend in eighth grade, and she knew that the pastor was lying on his application when he applied as youth pastor. It turned out he was a sex offender. She also knew something was wrong with Seth, but then, so did I," Ella says.

At the mention of Seth, Jason's body tenses. I think Ella does it to spite him some days. Jason can't stand that Seth almost ruined their wedding. I mean, he showed up in the church hours before and tried to shoot Jason. Thankfully, Jason and his brothers got him out, and the only thing ruined was a bouquet of flowers.

Ella squeezes Jason's arm. "He's locked up for a long time, and he can't hurt us." Ella soothes him, but it still takes a bit for Jason to relax again.

We get to the cabin at the end of the walking path, and we all stop.

"I always forget this is out here," Jason says.

"What is it?" I ask.

"Well, Sage would know more, since her family used to own this side of the ranch, but I know this was the first building ever built on this land. It was about thirty years after my family settled here. They lived in this cabin for a few decades, before they built the house you're staying in now. Then, her family lived there for two generations I believe, before the big house was built. When we bought the property back and merged the two ranches together, Sage had the main house completely remodeled. She didn't want any of the bad memories," Jason says.

"Why don't you guys restore this cabin?" Ella asks.

"That's up to Sage, and she never has wanted to. I don't know if she forgot about it, or if there's a reason she doesn't want to touch it. You'd have to ask her," Jason says.

We turn and slowly walk back to the house in no rush to get there.

"Oh, Maggie, before I forget. I need you to go over the menu with Nick and get it finalized, so I can get them printed up. Can you do that soon?" Ella asks. She won't look at me when she does it either.

"Soon, like tomorrow soon?" I ask.

"Oh yes, please. That would be perfect! You know Nick will be there for dinner at WJ's."

I shake my head. "You aren't fooling anyone, Ella. Least of all me."

Jason chuckles, but Ella tries to play innocent. "I have no idea what you mean."

Chapter 12

Nick

I love my half days at WJ's. They allow me to work my land a bit more. I don't have many animals here just a few cows, two horses, and some chickens. I'm getting a pen ready to bring in a few pigs.

I like raising my own food. You can't beat fresh eggs for breakfast. If I had the time, I'd start a vegetable garden, but the animals take up a good part of my time. I wonder if Maggie has any gardening interest. I know her sister Ella does, so maybe, Maggie will want to start a garden here one day.

I'm working on the fence for the pigpen, and my mind is on Maggie, so I don't hear the truck pull up until Jason leans over to give me a hand.

"Hey, I didn't expect to see you until tonight," I tell him.

"Well, I'm heading in a bit early and thought I'd stop by to talk to you. Have you been in town, since Sunday night?"

The bar is closed Mondays, which was yesterday, and only open for dinner Tuesdays and Wednesdays. Thursday through Sunday we serve lunch and dinner.

"No, I spent all day yesterday working on this pen to get ready for the pigs. Same as today," I tell him. It's Tuesday, so I doubt I missed anything big in town. Even gossip is slow at the beginning of the week in Rock Springs.

"It's a good thing you didn't, I guess. Ella and I had dinner at her parents' house last night, and Maggie went for a walk with us. She had an interesting encounter at the diner yesterday."

This stops me dead in my tracks. The fence forgotten as I turn to face Jason. "Is she okay?"

"Yeah, just a little shaken up, I think. She had lunch with Megan, and Lauren interrupted them."

"What? What's she doing here?"

"She came to see you and made it very well known. When she found WJ's closed, she got a room at the B&B and plans to be in tonight to see you."

"Shit. What the hell is she doing here?"

"Well, from the sound of Maggie and Megan's story, she's here to see you and wasn't very nice to Maggie. Several people were seconds from stepping in, and that's not the worst of it."

I knew Lauren was acting a little off when we had lunch at her place in Dallas, but I never gave her any reason to think I'd want her to visit me. She did try to flirt a bit during the competition, and I brushed her off. She has that mean girl vibe, that no matter how beautiful she is on the outside, it makes her really ugly on the inside. Those are the girls I stay as far away from as possible.

The fact that anyone was mean to Maggie doesn't sit well with me, and that she made the trip and went out of her way to be nasty to Maggie sets me on edge. Is this going to set Maggie and me back? I hope she doesn't think I'd invite her here. Wait, did Jason say there's more?

"How does it get worse?" I ask.

"Ella is playing matchmaker, and no matter what I say, she isn't listening. She told Maggie with less than a month to the dance that she needs your final menu to get them printed. So, she's sending Maggie to see you tonight at work."

"Damnit."

"Listen, for what it's worth, Maggie likes you, but she doesn't have a lot of dating experience, but she has killer gut instincts. She knows Lauren is trouble, and she doesn't do trouble. She'll walk away, instead of getting involved. If you plan to move forward with Maggie, you need to nip whatever this is with

Lauren in the bud, and then tell Maggie where you stand. It needs to be big, and it needs to be tonight. If there's any doubt in her mind, you might lose her for good. Just my observations."

Jason says his goodbyes and heads out, leaving me to think. I don't know why Lauren is here, but I guess I'll find out tonight.

· · · ● · ● · · ·

My mind has been distracted ever since I got to the bar today, waiting for Lauren to show up, and also waiting for Maggie to show up.

"NICK! What's wrong with you today? You're miles away." One of the kitchen staff says.

"Sorry. You guys okay in here? I'm going to go check on the bar."

"We got it, go!"

Jason and Ella are locked in his office going over last year's numbers and paperwork. Jason is really good with the accounting and is doing all the comparisons and getting the paperwork ready to get to the CPA for taxes. All that fun stuff.

I give the bartender a break, as we are slow enough right now. Making my way down the bar checking on everyone, I notice a new guy, sitting taking everything in. He holds up his beer bottle to me, and I grab him another one.

"New or passing through?" I ask him.

"New," he chuckles. "Everyone knows everyone here; you're the third person to ask."

"We're a small town and notice these things. I'm Nick, co-owner of this place."

That's the first time I've said those words, and it hits me. *Co-owner.* I own half of WJ's. At least I will, once we sign the paperwork next week. I own my own place. I never thought that would happen, because I never planned to leave Rock Springs, and this isn't exactly a place for a five star restaurant. So, when Jason approached me to start bringing food to the bar, I jumped at it. I knew Jo wouldn't have a need for me until she retires, and with how she's going, that won't happen for a few more years.

"My name is Evan, and I'm a new ranch hand in the area."

"Oh yeah, which ranch?" I ask, making conversation and hoping to make him more comfortable.

"I'm not at liberty to say. Part of my contract." He tells me.

I look him over. He's a little rough around the edges and has a tattoo that peaks out from under the sleeve of his shirt. His sandy blonde hair is just long enough that it curls under his hat.

I know some ranches around here will bring in guys on parole to help, and the contracts they have are very strict, so it's not an uncommon thing to not know where some guys are working right away, but it always comes out. Nothing stays a secret long here in Rock Springs.

"Well, you're always welcome so long as you stay out of trouble. Here and the diner across the way are the best places to get to know people. There's a Sweetheart's Dance next month and pretty much everyone will be there, so it's another great way to meet people. Maybe, you get a ticket for it."

"Thanks, I was curious. I'm hearing talk of abandoned horses at the church. Is that a joke?" He asks.

"No, we had a horse show up at the church Christmas Eve. It was from an illegal rodeo and racing we think. That one recovered well, but recently, we had another show up at a ranch here that takes in abandoned and abused horses. The horse is pregnant, and we aren't sure if either will make it just yet."

"Don't they normally kill those horses?" He asks me.

"That's what we understand. They've been dumping them around the county, which has the cops circling. My guess is they want the cops to think it's happening in the area, but it's probably set up west of here. The further west you go, the more open it is. You can pull up some back road and set up for months before someone stumbles up on you."

"What's out that way?" He asks.

"Nothing. Desert, mostly. Lubbock Texas is out there, and if you keep going, you'll hit New Mexico and Roswell."

"Sad situation. I hope they catch these guys soon."

"Me too. It's causing quite a stir here, and we like things a bit quieter."

He nods, and I move on to the far end to start with drinks.

The bartender comes back from break, and we are talking, when Lauren walks in. I don't think I realized just how much I was dreading this. She scans the place, and when her eyes land on me, her face lights up in a smile, and it makes my skin crawl. It's nothing like when Maggie smiles at me.

"Nick! Some place you got here." She tries to reach in for a hug, but I step back and offer her my hand. She shakes it, but eyes me up like I just grew a second head.

"What are you doing here?" I ask, trying to keep my tone friendly. No matter what anyone says, my momma would have a cow, if I wasn't polite.

"I was intrigued after you stopped by for lunch, so I thought it was only fair I come and check out your place." She sits down at a table near the bar. "Won't you join me for dinner?"

"No, who do you think is going to cook your food?" I ask her. "The waitress will be over to get your order. I need to go check on the kitchen."

I head straight to Jason's office and knock on the door. Ella opens it with a smile on her face, and her hair slightly disheveled. I know what happens in this office, and I try not to think about it. They are happy, and that's all that matters to me. I send up a silent prayer of thanks that, as a chef, I have my own office in the kitchen.

I step in, and Jason looks up from the paperwork. "Just wanted to let you know Lauren is here."

"Okay, I'll come out, and you can introduce us. We'll keep an eye on her, while you go cook her food," Jason says and pushes back from his desk.

"Do you know if Maggie is on her way?" I ask Ella.

"No, I don't babysit her." She rolls her eyes at me.

"If this backfires Ella, I'm blaming you. I don't care if you're her sister or Jason's wife. I'll blame you. Sending Maggie in here was low, and all it's going to do is hurt her." I storm out, not caring I just outed Jason.

I head right to the kitchen and straight to my office to gather my thoughts. The kitchen staff seems to have everything under control. Yes, I'm avoiding Lauren, I know that, and I don't care. I'm not sure how long I'm working on ordering supplies when Ella peeks her head in.

"Maggie's here." Ella's soft voice fills my office.

"Is Lauren still here?" I ask her.

She nods and actually looks sorry. I give her a pointed look and follow her out to the dining room.

I find Maggie, standing next to Lauren's table and talking to her. The look on her is southern evil sweet. Don't know what I mean by that? It's the face a southern woman gives that looks sweet, but it's dripping venom.

"Hey, Maggie." I lean in and hug her a little longer than necessary. "I had no idea she was going to be here," I whisper.

"I know." She whispers back, as she pulls away.

"Ella sent me to go over the menus for the dance," Maggie says this time for Lauren to hear.

"Of course, let's go to my office." But as I am walking by, Lauren grabs my wrist.

"I'd love a tour of the kitchen when I'm done." She smiles sweetly.

"Sorry, county regulations state no one in the kitchen who isn't on the insurance," I tell her.

"Well, she's going back." Lauren tilts her head towards Maggie. Thankfully, Ella hasn't left us yet and is quick on her feet.

"She's my sister, and since my husband owns the place too, she's permitted. Owner's family and employees only." Ella says, as I shoot her a look of thanks and try to convey that I'm not irritated with her anymore.

"Is there any age limit on the kitchen? Do you have to be at least sixteen to be in there, and what are you fifteen?" Lauren snaps.

"You don't listen very well, do you? Do you read?" Ella points to the sign above the bar that says.

'If you're an asshole, there will be a 25% service charge for dealing with you.'

And yes, we have a button on the system for it, and yes, we have used it before. In fact, we use it once a month at least. The ranchers who come into the bar in a shit mood just hit the button, before they order, or some even joke tonight's a 25% night and slap the button when they order. Then, the 25% goes as a tip to whoever has to wait on them.

"I don't think I'll see you before you go, so have a safe trip back to Dallas," I say just as Jason joins Ella. He always has an eye on her, and when she has to point to that sign, it's his silent call to come back her up.

I turn and take Maggie's hand, leading her to my office. I close the door and pin her to it.

"Dinner at my house. That will be our date. I'll cook all the food Jason won't let me make here. Then, I can show you the property, the animals, and the house. Say yes." I murmur a breath away from her lips.

"When?"

"This Saturday. I think Ella should have to work off the little stunt she pulled today, don't you?"

She giggles, and it wraps around my heart and holds me hostage. The sound is one I know I want to hear from her every day.

"Okay, I'll drive, though. I want to have my truck."

She wants a way to leave if things go too far or go sideways. Smart girl, I'll give her that.

"Of course." Then, my lips are on hers for a brief moment, before Ella pounds on the door.

"Lauren left. How are the menus coming along?"

I smile and open the door. "Oh, we need a bit more time, so we're going to meet at my place Saturday. You and Jason don't mind taking the bar over that night, right?" I smile.

Ella goes to open her mouth, I'm sure in protest when Maggie steps in. "Well, since we got distracted today with your matchmaking, I think it's only fair."

Ella's mouth snaps shut, and she purses her lips together, narrowing her eyes at us both.

"You will thank me someday." She says and storms off. No doubt to call Riley, who is the brains behind all this. That girl is the queen of the matchmakers. She has set out to make everyone in town as happy as she is.

"I better go." Maggie steps out of the office with a small smile.

I let her leave, knowing I'll have her all to myself this weekend.

Chapter 13

Maggie

As soon as I left the bar, I called Megan. I need an emergency girls' night. No moms, just Ella's sisters-in-law, Riley, Sage, Megan, and Sarah. Of course, Ella and Lilly will be there, too. Everyone who knows about how Ella and I were raised and about courting.

I haven't seen Sarah in a while, but I know Riley has been keeping her up to date on everything with Nick because she texts me telling me so.

Girls' night is always held at the house on the side of the property where Sage and Colt work. The guys go to Blaze and Riley's side of the house, where Blaze's parents still live. Tonight, Hunter's mom is hosting a mom's night at her place, where Helen and my mom are going to hang out, and the dads are going to a guys' night.

I guess, the moms sent food over, and the guys will play poker, and instead of money, they will bet candy and other food items. The most coveted items being their chips, using Helen's brownies.

I heard my mom say Helen and Donna were going to expose her to the movie *Magic Mike*. My poor mom.

So, that leaves us girls up to our own devices. Sage and Riley set up a taco bar for us. There are deserts and margaritas. I've only been to one other girls' night since Ella joined the family, and they are fun every time.

Everyone is here and has their plates of food. We ditched the dining room and are all curled up in the living room eating when Megan turns to me.

"It was Maggie who called this emergency meeting, so let her start the night off. We're here for you, girl with whatever it is."

I think my face turns bright red. It's hot, and I'm very nervous about this.

"Oh, she's turning red. This must be about Nick," Ella says gently.

This is what I love about these girls. This is a judgment-free zone, and they just want to help.

"Well, I'm sure you all know by now I'm not courting like Ella did," I say as I watch all the heads nod.

"I guess, I'm just out of my element and would like some perspective from those who know more about the dating world. We have a date at his place on Saturday."

"Wait, his place?" Sage asks. "Doing what?"

"Oh, he said dinner, and he wanted to show me the property and the house."

Everyone but Ella shares a look that I don't understand.

"How far have you gone with him so far?" Sarah asks.

"We've kissed a few times." I duck my head.

"Did you like him kissing you?" Sarah asks.

"Yes, more than I think I should have."

Everyone giggles and I'm not sure why, until Riley speaks.

"That's a good sign. When you feel like that from a kiss, then there's a good chance he could be the one."

"But generally, him inviting you to his house for dinner, means sex," Sage says.

My mouth drops open. "But we've only been on one other date, and it wasn't really a date."

My mind goes blank after that statement. He can't possibly, can he?

"Nick knows you and your situation. Chances are he wasn't thinking about sex, but truly about showing you his place, cooking for you, and taking care of you. You really need to figure out how far you want to go and let him know your boundaries. I know he'll respect them," Sage continues.

"What if I want..." I can't even bring myself to say it, but having his mouth on more than my lips, makes me feel hotter than I thought possible. His hands on my bare skin. Him inside me. I want that so much more than I want to admit.

"There's nothing wrong with wanting it, Maggie," Ella says. "We were raised to think there is, but that church was wrong. I couldn't go out and sleep with just anyone, but there's nothing wrong with it if this is what you want."

For whatever reason, I think I needed that reassurance from Ella of all people that what I want is okay. To know that this wasn't a huge mistake because I want Nick more than I thought I could. I didn't think it was possible to desire someone so much.

"Feeling better?" Megan asks, and I nod. "Good, because I have the next problem. Hunter wants to name the baby after his dad."

"Hank is a good name. Don't you like it?" Sage asks.

"The problem is his name isn't Hank, it's Gerald!" Megan cries.

We all laugh. Who knew Hank was a cover up for Gerald? Poor guy. How could Hunter want to name his son that?

"Do you know what you're having yet?" Sarah asks. "This might be a moot point if it's a girl."

"No, we don't, and he wants the names set, before we find out," Megan pouts.

"Why don't you call his bluff and come up with a horrible name for a girl?" Lilly asks. She's holding baby Lilly, who Riley named after her. Whenever they are in the same room, those two are attached at the hip, and no one can fight the baby away from her.

"Or just be honest and say it's a horrible name for a kid this day and age. Maybe, suggest it for a middle name?" Ella says.

"It wouldn't be so bad for a middle name," Megan agrees.

Ella looks at me, "Maybe, we should fill them in on Lauren and what happened. Never hurts to have a few more people on our side."

"Hey, we're family, and on your side, no matter what. Even if it means burying a dead body at three a.m. We have plenty of land, and no one would find her." Sage says with a perfectly straight face.

I agree. So, Ella fills them in on what happened, and they all agree she wasn't there with good intentions, but that Nick handled it well.

The night flows, as we talk about the dance, and who in town is going with who. We do some online dress shopping for the dance, and even I join in and have a few margaritas.

By the time the guys make it back to the house, Jason takes one look at me and suggests I stay in one of the guest bedrooms tonight, and I agree without so much as a fight.

• • • • ● • ● • • ·

Waking up, in a room that isn't yours, is a strange feeling. I've only had alcohol one other time, before last night, and it didn't leave my head pounding quite like this.

I lie in bed and think about last night. I love this family. Ella may have married into them, but they have accepted me with open arms, and it was so great to have them to talk to last night.

All I can think about over the next few days is my date with Nick. What boundaries do I want? What is he expecting? What am I going to wear?

Nick texts me several times a day. Sometimes, it's photos of a new food item on the menu, and sometimes, it's of his animals. He texted a photo of the finished pigpen today. He's so excited about it, and I'm excited to see the baby pigs he has coming.

He's getting them from a farm about an hour from here. Since my dad is going to pick them up for him, my mom is going too, and they are making a day out of it.

Friday, I spend the whole day obsessing over what to wear. Ella even lets me raid her closet, which turns into going through just about everyone's closets. Finally, by dinner, I have it narrowed down to three outfits.

Normal everyday attire of jeans and a nice shirt with boots, or leggings with a sweater dress and ankle boots is under consideration. The third pick is a long sleeve, deep purple maxi dress with a lace belt at the waistline. The neckline dips a bit lower than anything I've worn before, but it's still pretty modest. Everyone, even the guys, agree to go with the purple dress, and I have Sarah to thank for that.

The way they acted, you would think it was a huge contest, and Sarah was taking home a gold medal.

Chapter 14

Nick

Maggie is coming for dinner tonight. It's all I've been able to think about all day. I've cleaned the house twice. I've gone over the recipes for tonight three times, and then tripled checked that I have everything I need.

I have changed my outfit four times already and then styled my hair twice, only to go back to the way I wear it every day. I'm a mess. I don't think I've been this nervous for a date ever. Never really had an interest in dating either.

I try to focus my energy on the animals when there's a knock on the door. Just as my nerves were starting to calm, they skyrocket again.

When I open my door and see Maggie standing there, I can't breathe. Her blonde hair is done in loose curls, falling over her shoulder, and the dark purple dress she has on makes her look like a princess, standing in my doorway.

She gives me a shy smile and shifts her weight, and I realize I haven't said anything.

"Wow, Maggie. You look amazing." I still can't take my eyes off her, no matter how hard I try.

Her eyes run down my body, and my cock twitches. Having her eyes on me like this is turning me on. She takes in my dark, dressy jeans and a button down shirt. It's cowboy casual and as fancy as I get without a suit. I hope she likes it.

A slow smile creeps across her face. "You look amazing too, Nick." Her voice is soft and almost breathless.

Finally, my brain starts working, and I step back, allowing her to walk inside. She takes a look around the basic farmhouse living room, while I close the door and take her coat.

I kept the house bright, using white wood trim and a light wood floor. The house is a bit bare, and it needs a woman's touch. My mom has tried, but I insisted that the woman who touches my house will be my wife, and she seemed okay with that.

"Whatever you're cooking smells good." She smiles and turns back to me. It's like her gaze freezes me. All sensible thoughts leave my head for a brief moment.

"Thanks, it's a roast, and a new recipe I've been wanting to try out. Do you want a tour of the house?" I say, once my brain starts working again.

"I'd love a tour." She smiles at me, and my heart races.

I show her the living room, and down the hallway to the three bedrooms that I have set up, as a guest room, office, and gym.

"Someday, I picture these as kids' rooms, but they serve this purpose for now."

"Where will you move your gym to then?" There's a hint of amusement in her voice.

"Well, I'll finally finish up the shed closest to the house, and then move it and my office out there."

I take a chance and take her hand in mine, as I lead her across the house to the master bedroom. She gives my hand a squeeze, but she doesn't try to pull away, so I take it as a good sign.

The master bedroom is huge, and one of my favorite parts of the house. I have a king bed, and the room makes the bed look small. There's a sitting area by the windows and a window seat.

This is the area Maggie seems drawn, too. I stand in the doorway, not trusting myself to follow her into the room. Seeing her in this space feels right. Almost too right.

"With a few more pillows, this window seat would be perfect for reading." She says, as much to herself as to me, as she stands and looks out of the window. "It's beautiful with the snow covering the ground. I wish it snowed like this every year."

This year just before Christmas we had a huge blizzard. We haven't had this much snow in almost ten years. Just when we think it might melt, we get another few inches. It does make everything more beautiful, but we all know it won't be like this next year, so we enjoy it, while we can.

Maggie turns and makes her way to the small hallway with a huge walk in closet on either side. One where I have all my clothes and one that is empty, waiting for hers. I didn't realize it until she was standing in this room, but this house is waiting for her. I feel sucker punched in the gut realizing that, like I've been waiting for Maggie all along.

As she walks further down the short hall towards the bathroom, I slowly move, so I can still see her.

She runs her hand over the edge of the large, clawfoot tub, and I'm instantly thankful my mom made me put it in.

"I've always loved clawfoot tubs. We moved into the house I grew up in when I was six, and it didn't have a tub. So, whenever I visited a friend's house, I always took a bath. I love them."

"Well, anytime you want to use the tub, it's yours. It's meant to be used." She smiles and stares out of the window to the back of the house.

"Come on, I'll show you out back."

I take her hand, leading her to the back porch. From here, she can see everything, and we won't have to get out in the dirt.

"My parents have a place on that end of the property," I say, pointing to the right. "You can't see them, because it's way down. That's the pigpen I just built. You'll have to come back over when you aren't dressed in such pretty clothes, so you can spend some time with the baby pigs." I tell her.

"Oh, I'd love that!" There's a twinkle in her eyes, as she looks out. I point out the barn and the chicken coup. I also tell her about the few cows and horses I have, before leading her back inside to warm up.

We sit on the couch, and I know this is where I need to have a talk with her before things go any further.

"Maggie, I really like having you here in my house, but I don't want to push things that you don't want. I wanted to ask how you see us dating, because sweetheart, I plan to date you." I make my intentions clear.

Her eyes go wide for a brief second before she turns her head and looks away from me. I rub my thumb over the back of her hand that's still in mine, offering a bit of comfort.

"I want to go slow and get to know each other, like really know each other. I liked kissing, but I'm not sure how much further I want to go." She chews on her bottom lip, which drives me crazy because I want that lip between my teeth.

Reaching up, I use my thumb and pull her lip free, and then gently turn her face to look at me.

"We can go as slow as you want. If you ever think we're moving too fast, tell me to stop. When I kiss you, I tend to lose all rational thought, so if you're ever not sure just pull back. We'll slow down, okay?"

She nods, still not saying anything.

"As for dating, I agree that's why I asked you here. I like cooking, and I wanted to cook for you. Nothing else is expected. Now, the church is having their Valentine's Day festival next week. Would you like to go with me? I'm off Monday, and we can make an afternoon of it."

"I'd like that." She smiles at me.

"Will you join me in the kitchen, while I finish up dinner?" I ask.

"Can I help?" She asks as we make our way into the kitchen.

"You can help by sitting your cute butt right here and keeping me company," I tell her, as I lift her onto one of the bar stools that I have at the kitchen island.

As I start on the side dishes, I want to keep her talking.

"What do you want to know about me? Nothing is off limits." I tell her.

We talk about family, and what it was like growing up in Rock Springs. She tells me about her photography, and some of the trouble she and Ella used to get into growing up.

She helps set the table, as I finish up dinner, and I send up a silent prayer there are many more nights like tonight in our future. Just simple at home dinner nights.

Once we sit down, I watch her take her first bite, and the little moan she lets out goes right to my dick. Thank God we are sitting down, and she can't see me getting hard, as she enjoys the meal I just made her.

"Nick, this food is delicious! This recipe is definitely a keeper!"

"I'm glad you like it. Though, the next few meals might have to be BBQ." I figure this will be a good way to segue over to the news I got today.

"I have no problem with BBQ. Are you trying to find some new recipes?"

"Yeah, since I won the championship in Dallas, I've been invited to compete in two more this year. Plus, I get to return to Dallas. I still need to talk to Jason, but I think he'll agree to it."

"Nick, that's wonderful! Which ones? Where are they? What do you plan to make? I hope you'll let me come. I want to be there!"

Her rapid fire questions make me smile, but it's her statement at the end that has my heart racing. Having her by my side would be amazing. My mom and dad went with me to Dallas, and it was great to have their support. I know they will make the time for these too, but having Maggie there, would be even more special.

"Well, one is The World Championship BBQ Cooking Contest in Memphis, Tennessee. That's in May..." I don't get to finish before she lets out a squeal.

"Nick! A world championship? That's amazing!"

I shake my head, but I can't seem to wipe the grin off my face.

"Well, there's more." I pause and watch her watch me for a moment before I continue.

"I was also invited to The Jack Daniel's World Invitational BBQ Championship in October."

This time, when she lets out a squeal, she jumps and runs around the table and hugs me. I wrap my arms around her and pull her into my lap. She puts her arms around my neck, smiling big at me.

"I'm so proud of you, Nick. You are a talented chef." Her eyes cloud over, and her smile falters.

"What's on that mind of yours?" I whisper, tucking some hair behind her ear.

"Do you ever think of moving to a city like Dallas and working at a restaurant?"

Ahhh, she's worried about me leaving.

"I thought about it for a bit after school, and I even applied at a few in Dallas. I toured one when I interviewed, and it just wasn't what I pictured. I tossed around starting my own place. Then, one night over a few beers Jason and I got to talking and working with him just fit. I love it here, and Rock Springs is where I want to live and raise my kids. Being partners with Jason is perfect, and the championship just adds a bit of fun."

That seems to comfort her, and then it's like she realizes she's sitting on my lap and gets all nervous. She stands up and goes back to her seat. The next few moments we eat in silence, and I want the ease back to what we had earlier. Then, a game my parents liked to play with me as a kid pops into my head.

"So, tell me a random fact about you," I say, and the smile creeps back on to her face.

"I hate swimming in the ocean because I can't see what's around me."

"Sounds like there's a story there," I say.

"I went with my parents to a church in Florida, where my dad was speaking, and we spent a day at the beach. I got stung by three jellyfish. Haven't been in the ocean since. Your turn."

"I always wanted to have a joint bachelor and bachelorette party in Las Vegas, before I got married."

"Really?"

"Yes, a friend of mine had one, and then, I got really sick with the flu and couldn't go. The pictures he shared were amazing." I smile, remembering how mad I was at being sick that weekend.

"I never thought of it before, but there's quite a bit I'd love to see and do in Las Vegas, and I can see how it would be a fun weekend."

We finish dinner this way, and I find out she loves Brussels sprouts, but she hates eggplant. She went vegan for six months but decided she liked steak too much. She loves reading romance books and hates horror books and movies.

I admit to her I know nothing about cars because I was always in the kitchen with my mom. I don't like cats, but I always keep one in the barn to help with mice. And surprisingly, when I was younger, I hated BBQ.

She insists on helping clean the dishes, and the conversation flows so easily that by the time we sit back down on the couch, we are laughing and smiling.

"You are so beautiful, when you smile like that," I tell her.

Her lips part, and her breathing picks up, and I can't stop myself from leaning in for a kiss. She kisses me back, hesitant at first, then a switch flips, and her arms wrap around my neck, as she pulls me in close.

I deepen the kiss, letting her take the lead. This is her show, and I don't want to push her into something she doesn't want or isn't ready for. But at the same time, I really don't want to stop her from something she is ready for.

I'd love nothing more than to sit on the couch with her like this and make out all night and not take it any further than kisses. Just having her lips on mine is as easy as breathing, and it's all I can concentrate on, so I don't realize she has crawled into my lap until she grinds down on me.

It's like a bucket of cold water thrown on the moment. I want her so badly that stopping here is one of the hardest things I've ever had to do, but I want to make sure she understands what she's doing to me.

"Mags, sweetheart, you do too much of that, and I won't be able to stop myself from taking this further than kissing."

She whimpers and grinds on me again, a bit more hesitantly. "I want to go further than kisses. I want you." She whispers in my ear.

There's no way this sweet, innocent girl has any idea what she's doing to me right now.

"Do you know what that means, Maggie?"

She nods, "I want more than kissing. I need you." She almost begs.

"No sex tonight, Maggie," I say in a stern voice, even if she thinks she's ready, I know she isn't.

"No sex. I promise to stop you when we hit my limit."

I swear she gives me a pout, and I'm done. I flip her over, so her back is on the couch, and I'm over her. I'm going to put that promise to the test.

I kiss her, and then make my way down her neck. She throws her head back for easy access, and as my lips move down, my hand moves up her thigh and under her dress. When my hand makes it to her silk underwear, I run my finger over her slit, and the fabric is soaked.

When she gasps, I freeze.

"Don't stop." She says as she raises her hips.

I rub her clit over her panties, as I pepper her collarbone with kisses.

"More," she gasps.

I'm sure she doesn't know what she needs more of, but I know what kind of more I want.

"Maggie, baby, I want to taste you." She looks at me, her eyes a bit glazed. "I want to put my mouth on you here." I run my finger under her panties, skin on skin, and almost cum in my pants, as her wetness soaks my fingers.

Her hips buck, and she moans, but it's not the yes, I need.

"Can I, sweetheart?" I ask again, and this time her eyes meet mine.

"Yes, Nick, please!" She whines, and if how wet she is, is any indication, then she's close.

I sit up and slide her panties down, placing them in my pocket. These babies I plan to keep, a memento from not just Maggie's first time having a man's mouth on her, but her first time having my mouth on her. I made her soak them, so I'm keeping them.

I push her dress up her waist and get my first view of her perfect, pink pussy, and seeing it glisten with her cream, has me ready to cum. I move down and stop her, as she tries to close her legs.

"Keep them open. You are so damn perfect, Maggie, and so wet for me, that's a huge turn on." I reassure her.

She relaxes back into the couch, and I spread her thighs, and then take my first long lick of her pussy.

She cries out my name, as her back arches. She's so close, as her pussy is pulsing, trying to reach out for my cock, which it wants more than it wants my tongue.

I latch on to her clit and don't let up between sucking and licking. Maggie is very vocal about what she likes, and I love it. Just having my mouth on her, has me so hot that

I'm humping the couch for a bit of relief. I don't remember ever being this hard.

I push my luck, and while I flick her clit with my tongue, I slowly insert a finger into her. She's so tight that I'm worried I might hurt her. After only a few thrusts, I hook my finger and hit the spot I was looking for. Her whole body locks up, and she pulls my hair, pulling me closer, as she cums.

Feeling her pussy gripping my finger so tight, and thinking about it around my cock, is my undoing. I cum in my pants, and my groan seems to make her cum harder. I have never seen anything more beautiful than Maggie letting herself go like this for me.

I lick her cream up; I think I'm addicted to it now. Then, I pull her dress back down and climb up her to find her eyes closed, and a huge satisfied grin on her face.

I lightly kiss her cheek, and her eyes pop open.

"Nick, that was incredible," she sighs.

"Watching you was amazing. Stay here and don't move. I need to clean up, and then, I plan to cuddle you." I stand up, and her eyes go to my crotch. I look down and see the wet spot there. "Yes, sweetheart, you did that to me."

I wink at her and jog to my room, where I clean up and change in record time. I don't want to miss a moment with Maggie. Walking back into the living room and seeing Maggie in an orgasm coma on my couch, I know I won't be able to stay away from her because now, I'm addicted to her.

I crawl on to the couch, pulling her to me, and she wiggles and gets comfortable.

"I love cuddling," she sighs.

"I love cuddling with you." I kiss the top of her head.

I think I'd love doing anything with her.

Chapter 15

Maggie

I'm lying in bed awake thirty minutes before my alarm goes off. I barely slept the last few nights, because all I could think about was what Nick did to my body on our date, and how I didn't want to stop.

I've run every moment over and over in my head, and I'm so turned on I could scream. Today is our date for the Valentine's Day festival, and I know spending the whole day around him feeling like this, is going to make me want to drag him back to his place for more.

I wonder if this is how Ella felt around Jason every time they were together. No wonder she needed a chaperone on every date. Then again, I'm sure she didn't do what Nick and I did before she was married. I've debated going and talking to her about this, but I don't think I could find the words. Plus, I like this being just between me and Nick. I don't want to bring someone else into our bubble just yet.

Last night, I stayed up thinking about what if things don't work out with Nick and would I regret what I did. The answer I came to was no, I wouldn't. I also don't think I'd regret going further with him either, which leads to me today.

I dress warm, since most of the festival is outside, and there's still snow on the ground. Jeans, boots, a flannel shirt, and my coat. I put my hair in a side braid Ella taught me to do and head downstairs. I'm too nervous to eat anything. Plus, I heard there will be some great fair food.

Nick was asked to do a table this year. He said he made some easy recipes and will have some of the kitchen staff there working. I guess, one of the guys is saving to go to culinary school, so he always jumps, when Nick has extra work for him. Nick won't admit it, but I think he makes up work now and then just to help him out.

Nick insisted he pick me up, like a real date, so I head up to the main house and sit down on the front porch, waiting for him. Ella joins me on the porch swing, and we sit in silence for a bit.

"Was it hard to be around Jason and not want to kiss him and have your hands all over him?" I finally ask her.

"Yes, but now that we're married, kissing, and doing all that stuff, I imagine it would be even harder."

I just nod, keeping my eyes on the drive away, but this is Ella. She can read me like a book.

"Something happened with you and Nick." It's not a question, so I don't bother denying it.

From the corner of my eye, I can see her studying my face. "Did you go all the way?" She asks gently.

"No, but I wanted to. And I still want to."

"What stopped you?"

"He did."

She nods and smiles. "He's a good guy. He doesn't want you to regret anything, which means he's serious about you. Don't push too hard. You have to go at his pace, too."

I let that sink in. I was so focused on what my limits were that I didn't think about his. Before we can talk any more, Nick's truck rounds the corner, and I jump off and run off the porch.

"Thanks, Ella," I call back over my shoulder. Nick stops the truck and gets out, as I throw my arms around his neck. He catches me and swings me around.

"How is it that it's only been forty-eight hours, but I missed you like crazy?" He asks when we pull back.

"I was thinking the same thing," I say, while he leads me to the other side of the truck and helps me in.

Once he climbs in, he pulls me across the bench seat up next to him. "Much better." His voice is rough, as he turns the truck around, and we head into town. His hand holds mine the entire way, as we talk about what we did yesterday.

One full day apart, and we are acting as if it's been months like we missed so much.

As we get closer to town, the buzz is contagious. This is the first day of the festival, and it will run all week, but it looks like the whole town is here. It seems that no one wants to be the last one to know what's going on.

"Megan texted me earlier and said we could park behind her shop and walk over. It'll be better than the parking they have for the festival," I tell him. He squeezes my hand, as we make our way behind Megan's shop.

I've been trying not to think about how the left side of my body is pressed to his, and how there isn't an inch between us. But once he parks, opens his door, and steps out, I feel cold and lost without him.

He leans into the truck and wraps his hands around my waist, picks me up, and sets me on my feet outside the truck. Then, he tucks my hand in his, and we make our way to the festival.

As we near the church, a buzz of activity fills the air. I can't keep the smile off my face as we enter the festival.

"What do you want to do first?" He asks me.

I take in all the booths, the games, and the rides. This is my favorite part of small towns. When they throw a festival, they know how to do it right.

"Let's start with the rides," I say.

"The Gravitron was always my favorite as a kid," Nick says.

He gets in line to buy tickets, as I check out The Gravitron ride that goes in a circle and makes wave movements with lots of lights and music. I take it all in, mesmerized by it all. Then, the ride starts to move backward, and the squeals of laughter fill the air, and I can't wait for our turn.

As we wait in line, Nick stands behind me and wraps his arms around my waist. He whispers in my ear, "The best part of this ride is that gravity throws you together with whoever you're riding with."

When the ride slows to a stop, I watch everyone exit, and my nerves shift into high gear. When we used to go to the fairs and festivals back home, I would always ride with Ella. This will be my first ride with a guy.

Nick hands over our tickets to the ride operator, and we head to our seat. He pulls the bar down, and as it clicks into place, the excitement I feel ramps up into high gear. Energy fills the air, as everyone fills the seats.

The ride attendant gives his safety speech, and then, the ride slowly starts to creep forward. With each passing moment, it begins to gain speed. Suddenly, I'm thrown against the side wall of our seats, and Nick is being pressed to my side.

Laughter escapes me, and I'm smiling so hard that my cheeks hurt. I don't remember the ride ever being this fun before. Nick has one arm over my shoulder, trying to hold his weight up against the side, so he doesn't crush me, but his smile matches mine.

As the ride slows, his gaze on me gets intense. He leans in, and his lips touch mine for just a brief second before the ride starts moving backward. This time it's him who is thrown up against the side wall and me who is pressed up against him. I'm laughing too hard to be able to hold my weight off of him, so he wraps his arms around me.

When the ride slows to a stop, I can't remember the last time I've laughed so hard. When Nick removes his arms from around my waist, I feel cold again. I want his warmth back.

He helps me out of the ride, and still a bit dizzy, I sway against him, causing every inch of my body touching his to be set on fire. Being so close to him is intoxicating, but the moment is broken, when another couple getting off the ride bumps into us.

Nick looks around, then leads me to the exit and around the side of the ride. In the shade, away from all the prying eyes, he backs me up to the side of the building. His eyes are locked with mine, and he's breathing as heavy as I am.

He moves closer to me, and inch by inch, my heart starts racing more, and I send up a silent prayer, hoping he's going to kiss me. The need to kiss him is overwhelming, almost more than the need to breathe.

As he gets closer, his warm breath caresses my lips, and I lean forward, closing the gap between us. When our lips meet, the sizzle is intense. He grips my waist and flattens me back against the wall. He leans into me so close there isn't an inch of space. I can feel his heart racing against his chest, and I'm sure he can feel mine.

His other hand curls around the back of my head, pulling me even closer to deepen the kiss. When his tongue slides against my lips seeking entrance, I give it to him.

His tongue tangles with mine in long, slow strokes. It seems like the world stops spinning, and nothing else seems to exist. I don't hear anyone around us, and I don't feel time passing. The kiss goes on forever, yet, it ends too soon. Finally, Nick pulls away, resting his forehead on mine, as we both catch our breath.

"I think we should go check out the food." He says, his voice gruff, and his gaze on me is intense.

I nod and let him lead me towards the smell of fried food and sweets.

"What is your carnival food weakness?" He asks. "Mine is always tacos. I like trying the new versions they make every year."

"The fried desserts. Oreos, Kit Kat bars, and last year, the fried Swiss Cake Rolls and Pop Tarts. They were pretty good."

Nicks laughs, as his eyes roam the food booths. "Well, I should make you eat something resembling a meal before I feed you all those sweets. I'm going to be slightly biased and swing by WJ's booth, so you can try our food first."

Three tacos, half a Philly cheesesteak, two fried Oreos, a fried Kit Kat bar, and an ice cream cone later, I'm so full I think I'm going to burst.

"Let's walk the grounds, and maybe, play a few games to walk off the food," he suggests, taking my hand and heading towards where the games are set up.

We leisurely walk the rows of games and watch many people we know try their luck at this game or that. Many of the other couples are doing the same as us, and a rush of warmth floods over me. We are a normal couple.

A few years ago, I thought I'd never have this. I thought I'd be forced into a courtship with some guy from our church. I'm not sure what Jason said or did to bring this change in Mom and Dad's mind, but I'm forever grateful for the way him finding Ella shifted our lives.

"Come on, let's ride The Ferris Wheel." Nick pulls me towards the large wheel, and my nerves instantly hit me.

Nick can read me like a book, and he stops in his tracks and studies my face.

"What is it?" He asks gently.

"It's the heights. I always took Ella on The Ferris Wheel, it's her favorite, but the height gets me every time."

"I promise you, nothing will happen to you. I'll hold you in my arms the whole time. But if you don't want to go, then that's fine, too."

Every year, I watched The Ferris Wheel, and at the top, I watch couple after couple kiss. I always dreamed of my own Ferris Wheel kiss. Of course, I assumed it would be my husband when I finally got my turn.

I pull Nick towards the line. "I always wanted my own Ferris Wheel kiss at the top."

Nick smiles, as we wait for our turn to board the ride. He can't seem to keep his hands off of me, and I find I don't want him, too. As we take our seats, my nerves return, and like he promised, he wraps his arms around me and pulls me close against him.

I grab hold of the bar in front of us, as the ride lurches and starts its climb. As we climb in the air, we get a bird's eye view of not just the festival, but downtown, too.

"You know Pastor Greg places The Ferris Wheel in this same spot every year?" He whispers in my ear.

The heat of his breath against my ear sets a whole different set of nerves into gear. I forget we are rising above the ground until he speaks again.

"He says this is the perfect spot, because of the view right down Main Street. Open your eyes, sweetheart, you don't want to miss this."

I open my eyes, and he's right, the view right down Main Street is like one of those picturesque small-town photos. The Texas landscape beyond that is breathtaking.

"Wow," I gasp because words escape me.

Nick tightens his hold on me, as we reach the top of the ride, and it slows to a stop. I turn my head and look at him, and he wastes no time leaning in for a gentle kiss that takes my mind off the height. How his kisses make me forget everything else, I have no idea.

As the ride lurches and starts our descent back down to the ground again, the kiss ends, and the world sweeps back in. I find with his arms around me the nerves over the height and ride aren't there.

All I am able to focus on is Nick, and I find I can enjoy the ride. I trust he will keep me safe, and that safety is one I now crave. Knowing someone has your back no matter what, and there's another person on your side, is a feeling Ella has tried to describe to me before, but I couldn't grasp it before. *I get it now.*

As we get off the ride, Nick turns to me. "Want to head back to my place for a bit?"

I nod, and we go to his truck. The ride to his place flies by, and before we know it, we are pulling up in front of his house. I know what I want, and I decided on the way here I'm going to get it.

The moment we are in the door, I pull Nick towards me in a demanding and deep kiss. He doesn't miss a beat, pushing me up against the door, as his hard length presses into my belly.

His hands run down the sides of my body, and with every inch, his touch makes me want him even more. I want more of what we did on the couch, but I want so much more than what we've already done.

When his hands reach my ass, they grab hard and pull me up off my feet. Instinctively, I wrap my legs around his waist, putting my core right against the bulge in his pants. He starts walking, and I grind against him.

"You keep grinding that wet pussy against me, and we won't make it to the bedroom, sweetheart." He growls in my ear.

That's when I realize we are in the short hall, leading to his room. No sooner than we enter his room, my back hits his bed. He pulls my ass to the edge, and in no time flat, he has my shirt off and is working on my jeans. My mind clears enough to help him remove my jeans.

Lying on the bed in just my bra and underwear, his eyes rake over me from head to toe and back again.

"You have entirely too many clothes on there, cowboy," I say, and that spurs him into action. Without wasting any time, he stands before me in nothing but his boxer briefs.

"I wish I could tell you I'm going to drag this out for hours, but you knew exactly what you were doing on those rides today. We just had hours of foreplay, and I don't think I can take even a few more minutes." He says with his heated eyes still running over my body.

I know exactly what he means, so I sit up and remove my bra. "So, what are you waiting for?" I tease him.

That little question is enough to kick him into gear. He rips my panties off and sheds his boxer briefs before he heads over to his nightstand and gets a condom. I always knew the point of condoms, but I never thought of them as sexy, until right now. Watching Nick roll the condom onto his cock, in almost slow motion, is one of the sexiest things I've ever seen.

The moment he is done, he has me in his arms and pulling me to him. Bracing himself over me, his eyes meet mine, and his hand trails down, playing with my clit. Then further down, as he slides a finger into me. The sensation is delicious.

"So, wet for me. Need to stretch you out, so I don't hurt you. I want you so bad." He murmurs against my skin, as he adds a second finger. When his thumbs start playing with my clit, I don't even get a warning, as the climax washes over me. As soon as I start to relax, he moves over me, and I'm ready to go again.

His eyes are locked with mine, as the tip of his cock rests outside of my entrance.

"You're mine, Maggie. From this moment on, I'm yours and you're mine."

"Yes," I agree.

He slowly starts sliding his cock into me, making short shallow thrusts, as he stretches me. The stretching feels incredible, and my eyes start to roll back into my head until he hits my barrier and freezes. We both look at each other, almost frozen in time.

"I don't want to hurt you, but I promise to take the pain away." He whispers and then leans down to kiss me. It's an all-consuming kiss and one that has me forgetting about what he's about to do. When he thrusts forward breaking through my hymen, the pinch of pain causes me to dig my nails into his back, and I gasp.

He never breaks the kiss, and once he's fully inside me, he pauses and lets me adjust, before starting another slow rhythm. One that I match him thrust for thrust. What is slowly building feels bigger than anything I've ever experienced.

He pulls back, and his eyes lock with mine again, and it's not just us chasing our release, but our souls connecting. They are intertwining and molding together in a way that I know I will never be able to get out of my system.

His hands are all over me, but when he reaches between us and strums my clit, all my nerve endings explode, as I scream Nick's name. The room disappears, and I hear and see nothing but Nick, who grunts my name before his body locks up with his climax.

As he relaxes, he rolls us to the side and peppers my face with gentle kisses.

"That was amazing, sweetheart. Thank you for giving me that precious gift. I've never felt anything so perfect." He whispers against my skin.

"Mmm, Nick. That was perfect. I had no idea it could be like that." I sigh, happily content to not move the rest of the night.

He chuckles, as he stands up. "It was perfect because it was us. I've never felt anything like that before."

I know he's been with other girls, so when he says that, my heart races, thinking we are something special, and knowing he feels it too means everything.

He comes back with a warm washcloth to clean me up, before joining me back in bed. This cuddling thing is dangerous. Minutes after he pulls me into his arms, I am out.

Chapter 16

Nick

It's been a couple of days since Maggie and I were at the Valentine's Day Festival. She spent the last two days with me at my place, since I didn't work, and she went home today to get ready for this meeting about the Sweetheart's Dance.

Ella wanted them to drive in together and chat. I assume it's all that sister and girl talk the girls do. I assume that Ella will know every detail by the time she gets here today, which means, Jason will know by tonight.

I don't regret one moment with Maggie, but I know Jason will be protective of her, so I have a feeling a talk is coming.

I finish up placing this week's food order for the kitchen and head out to the main dining room just as Ella and Maggie walk in laughing arm in arm. Maggie's eyes light up when she sees me, and Ella's smile also widens, so I guess, all they talked about was good.

Maggie floats into my arms and kisses me in front of Ella and Jason, before pulling me to the table to sit with her for the meeting.

Everything is complete now that I have her back in my arms again, even though, it's only been a few hours. I feel whole now that she's here. I hated her leaving me this morning, even knowing I'd see her in a few hours.

I spent the entire time I was getting ready to come in, trying to figure out how I could convince her to move in with me. I kept coming to the same conclusion. In order to respect her and her family, she's going to have to marry me first.

The thought of marriage doesn't scare me anymore like it used it. Thinking of marrying Maggie is something I'm excited to look forward to. I'd ask her today if I thought she'd say yes.

Jason gives me a weird look, one that's a bit hard to read, before he looks over at Ella's face, and his face lights up.

I know that feeling of pure happiness; it's how Maggie makes me feel when I'm around her.

We go over details for the dance, decorations, and food. Then, we also figure out the volunteer list and assign them duties.

From the looks of it, I think we are pretty well ready for the dance, and I can't wait to be there with Maggie.

When the meeting is over, I take Maggie back to my office. I sit on the couch and pull her on to my lap.

"You'll go with me to the dance, right?" I know we have mentioned it, but I want to make sure I've officially asked her.

She smiles and kisses my cheek.

"If I'm going, I'm going with you."

I kiss her on the lips, and what was meant to be a soft, short kiss, turns steamy, when she turns and straddles me.

"I need you," she whispers against my lips.

"Not here, sweetheart."

Anyone could walk in at any time, and I won't have anyone but me seeing her like that. She left my bed this morning satisfied, so knowing she needs me as much as I need her makes the caveman in me pound my chest.

Her little pout indicates I need to give her some form of relief. I grip her hips and pull her over my erection, making her gasp.

She has leggings and a large sweatshirt on, so I know she can feel how hard I am against the ridge of my jeans. She tries to move faster, but I tighten the grip on her hips, keeping a slow and steady pace.

I keep kissing her, sucking her tongue into my mouth, and making love to her mouth at the same pace she's gliding across my cock.

Her breathing picks up, and knowing she's close, I stretch out her climax, before I thrust my hips up to hers, providing enough friction for her to fall over the edge. I kiss her hard, muffling her cries until she starts to relax against me.

She rests her head on my shoulder, and I rub her back, enjoying having her close to me.

This is one memory I will think of every time I walk into this office. It's going to be a fight not to get hard at work, thinking about what we just did on the couch, but it was completely worth it.

A knock on the door breaks the calm, and Maggie jumps like she has something to hide. I wrap my arms around her even more and adjust her, so she isn't straddling me, but sitting next to me.

"Yeah?" I call out.

The door opens, and Jason peeks his head in.

"Sorry to interrupt, but there's someone here who needs to talk to us."

Maggie stands up and straightens her clothes. The slight flush on her cheeks only makes her look even more stunning.

"Ella and I should get going anyway. We promised to help Sage with dinner tonight."

I stand, giving Maggie a peck on her cheek before she heads out. Jason looks at me and shakes his head, before heading back to the dining room.

Following him, I see a man who looks like he could be a ranch hand on any ranch around town. His boots are dirty, his jeans are well used, but the flannel shirt looks new, and the cowboy hat on his head is a bit newer than most.

"Come back to my office, and we can talk privately there," Jason says, and we both follow him to the back of the building. When Jason locks the door behind us, I start to realize this isn't just your normal meeting.

"This is my partner, Nick, and he's the chef here. The ladies you saw leaving were my wife and her sister, Nick's girlfriend. Nick, this is Ken. He's a state trooper and wants to come in undercover on the illegal rodeo case."

I nod, "What does that have to do with us?"

"Well, we know small towns don't have many secrets. We also know they don't share those secrets with outsiders. If I can come in undercover, then maybe, people will be open to talking to me. This could help in finding the missing links in the case. I'd also like you two to keep your eyes and ears open. It's a bar, people drink, and things tend to slip. Miles told me you two could be trusted."

I don't realize I let out a growl when he mentions Miles until both men are looking at me.

Ken looks at Jason for an answer, and he laughs.

"Miles made a move on his girl when he first got here. It's been settled, but it would be best to keep Miles away from Maggie."

Ken nods and then moves on.

"Have you heard of anything going on recently?"

"Well, I can't say I have, but I also haven't been looking all that hard either," Jason admits.

"The other night I was tending bar, and a new guy was at the bar. He didn't say much, and he was just watching everyone. Kelli tried to hit on him, and he brushed her off. He wouldn't say where he was working, just that he was newly hired, and it was against his contract to disclose where."

"It's not uncommon though around here. Some ranches like to keep things private around my family. They see us as big competition, so if they're doing anything new, they don't like the word to get out."

"Why your family?" Ken asks.

"Usually because we are the second biggest ranch in the state. Sometimes, it's simply because we work with the Native American reservation outside of town, and some families still don't get along with them."

Ken makes some notes in a notebook and asks some questions about the guy I saw the other night. He asks about events and busy times here at the bar, too.

"Listen, my family's ranch has a lot of older cabins away from everyone. We can say you're there helping fix some of them up, and you're staying in one. That way you'll be out of the eyes of the ranch hands. Gives you a legit reason for being in the area, and if you say you're working for my family, no one will question it," Jason offers.

"Can we not tell anyone there what's going on?" Ken asks.

"Well, we need to tell my brother, Blaze, and my sister, Sage. They run the ranch and will question it, but they're trustworthy and will be able to help point you in any direction you need. Anyone who works at the ranch is welcome to eat at the main house, and my other sister, Megan, owns the beauty salon in town, and it's gossip central. She's the one to talk to regularly, just don't upset her husband, while doing it. Her husband's mom would be a good source for the church gossip ring as well."

"Everyone seems to know everyone here, huh?" Ken asks.

We both agree, and he shakes his head.

"How do you know Lilly and Mike?" Ken asks.

Jason answers that one, "Mike was our senior ranch hand, and Lilly is best friends with Riley, my brother Blaze's wife. They're basically family."

Ken laughs again. "I hope to find a town like this to settle down in one day. I always thought they went the way of Mayberry, but I'm glad to see they are still around."

Ken stands and shakes both our hands. "Okay, I'll be at the ranch tomorrow, and we can make the introductions. I'll be here Friday night if you can introduce me to a few key people. Also, if I'm here and that guy comes back in Nick, will you let me know?"

"Of course," I agree.

We walk him out, and then Jason turns to me.

"This is a bigger issue than even I thought it was."

I can agree to that, and I'm hoping that we'll catch these guys fast before Rock Springs gets pulled in more than it already is.

Chapter 17

Nick

Today, we are having one of the last normal days, before the hectic week of the Sweetheart's Dance takes over. The town is already decorating in red, pink, and white. Every shop, office, and even the church.

On our normal date, Maggie asked to see more of my family's land. We decided to go horseback riding, and that way I can show her some of my favorite places on the ranch.

She said she was going to stop at the diner and get some stuff for us to have a picnic lunch. I keep checking the time and my phone for any news from her. I've been up since sunrise, looking forward to her visit. It's exciting to show her the land that means everything to my family.

When I went to culinary school, my parents supported me, but they were a bit disappointed too, even if they wouldn't admit it. My dad wanted me to take after him and run the ranch.

A few years ago, we sat down and talked. I assured them I didn't want to lose the ranch, and I planned to live on this land and have a foreman help me with running it. I'm hoping my wife will love the land and want to help take care of it, too.

That's why today is such a big day. I want Maggie to fall in love with my land. To want to live here and raise our kids here, because I realized over the last few days, that she's it for me. She will be my wife, and if she doesn't love this land as I do and doesn't want to run it, then we have to come up with a Plan B.

I know she wants to be a photographer, and I would never ask her to give that up. In fact, I have plans to build a photography studio on the property. She can spend her days on the land taking photos to share with the world. Her clients could come out and have pictures done. I think city people from Dallas would pay good money for a good old-fashioned Texas photoshoot.

I look at my phone again and still nothing. After breakfast, I went to the barn and made sure the horses and all the tack were ready for our ride. I checked it three times to be sure. I've cleaned the house and made sure dinner was ready to go into the oven when we got back.

She should be here any time, and I can't stop my nerves from getting the best of me.

The last two nights she's spent at her parents' home, which means the last two nights she wasn't in our home. In our bed. In my arms. It's made me a bit restless.

So, I head out to the front porch and start pacing impatiently, as I wait for her. It seems like forever, until she's pulling into the driveway. The trail of dust behind her truck blows in the wind, and as she gets closer, I can see the wide smile on her face.

I'm at her door, before she even puts the truck in park, and when the door opens, she launches into my arms. I'm finally calm now that she's right where she is meant to be.

"Oh, I've missed you! But Lilly can only cover for me for so long without raising my parents' suspicions. As amazing as they have been, I still don't think they'd approve of me staying the night here."

I kiss her forehead and breathe her in. She's here in my arms, and that's all I need. For now.

"It's okay. You have to spend time with your family, too. Time apart is good for us." I tell her.

"I've tried telling myself that, too."

I walk her inside, so she can set her stuff down, and it's then I notice a picnic basket. Maggie sees me looking at it, as a slight blush crosses her cheeks.

"Jo, at the diner, made that for us. Basket and all. I'm going in later this week to shoot the photos for her new menu and to use them on her website. I'm really excited."

Her smile grows bigger the more she talks about her photo shoot at the diner.

"It's perfect. Let's get ready and head out. I can't wait to show you around."

Walking hand in hand out the back door, I lead her over to an area beside the garage.

"I was thinking, I could build you a photography studio here. You can design it any way you want. If you want an area where you can have clients come out for photo shoots, a work area, and a storage area for props, you decide. Whatever you want, we can make happen."

I can see with her far off gaze that she's lost in the thought of her own studio, and I hope she starts planning it, because I can't wait to give it to her.

"That sounds like long term plans there, Nick." She tries to make a joke of it, bumping her shoulder into mine.

"Well, that's because I'm thinking long term, Maggie. This isn't just some fling for me. I'm very serious, and I want you to know that."

Her face goes soft, and she nods, turning towards the barn and changing the subject.

"Show me these horses you have gotten me all excited about."

I'll let her change the subject for now. I know I need to ease her into this, and I can be patient. I don't want to scare her off after all.

We make our way to the barn, and she takes in everything. We stop and see the baby pigs, which are mostly resting and calm. She snaps a few pictures with her phone, before we head into the barn.

We get the horses ready, and she impresses me by saddling her horse all on her own. I check it over, and it's done perfectly.

"Sage and Riley have been teaching me how to be a real cowgirl. Colt even taught me how to drive the tractor, so I can help during the spring Hell Week, when they get the ranch ready for summer."

She's almost bouncing off her feet with excitement about being able to help at the ranch. Hell Week happens twice a year, once in the spring to check the new calves and separate cows for the summer. They get the fields ready as well. Then again in the fall, when they check the cows and separate them out again. Finally, they get the hay ready and winterize the ranch.

It's some crazy days where they work from sun up to sundown, and Jason even helps out. I take over WJ's, while he's working with his family.

They bring in extra help from the reservation. Their family is close with the

Native American tribe, since Jason's brother, Mac, is from the reservation.

His parents adopted Mac, Sage, and Colt as kids when they needed a place to go. They always encouraged Mac to stay close to the tribe and work very closely with them.

We mount the horses and head out. While we walk the horses along the pasture behind the barn, Maggie tells me about all the talk of the dance in town.

"I feel sorry for Pastor Greg, because the little old ladies are trying hard to set him up with a date to the dance, but he says he's going alone. They're whispering that he has his eye on someone, but no one knows who."

I chuckle. Pastor Greg is in his mid-twenties, and ever since he came and took over the church in town, the church ladies took it upon themselves to help marry him off. He's been fighting them for two years now, but they won't give up.

"When he finds the right girl, he'll know, and they better lay off him then."

"Oh, they will. It's all with good intentions. They want him happy. I think they would do it to any single guy, you included, if you had stayed single much longer," she jokes.

"Then let's make sure they get the word out that I'm taken, and I'm very happy about it." I smile over at her.

She smiles back, as we enter the tree line. There's a path here that leads to a clearing that will be perfect for a picnic. It's narrow, so she trails behind me, making it difficult to talk.

I take a deep breath of the fresh Texas air and close my eyes, taking it all in. My horse knows this path as well as I do, so she'll stay on it, and I can relax. I listen to the clip-clop of the horses on the path and the dried leaves and twigs, snapping beneath their feet.

The weather has warmed up a bit, and the snow has started to melt, and when the sun peeks through the trees, I can feel it warming my face.

As we near the clearing, I call over my shoulder to Maggie, "I think we should eat right up here. It's one of my favorite spots on the property."

"Okay," she calls back, as we clear the tree line. It's not much with the dead grass in the center, where the sun has melted the snow. There's still snow on the ground around the edges of the meadow, where the trees shade it from the heat of the sun.

As my feet touch the ground, I feel at home again. I help Maggie off her horse, and no sooner than her feet touch the ground, do I spin her and have her back up against a tree.

My lips find hers in the same second, and her warm breath dances across my face. Her tongue meets with mine, as I press my body against hers. Her hands at the back of my neck pull me in closer, and I smile against her lips. Knowing she wants me as much as I want her, calms my soul.

As I pull back, she lets out a small whimper and tries to pull me back to her.

"Soon, sweetheart, I promise."

I turn and gather the horses to tie off to the tree just to be safe, and Maggie grabs the lunch and blanket we brought.

As we spread out in the sun, I'm already making plans to bring her back out here in the spring, when the flowers start to bloom.

"In the spring and summer, there are some of the most colorful wildflowers here. Blue, purple, orange, red, and yellow. We'll have to come back; it makes an even better picnic spot then." I tell her.

"It's a date." She smiles, as she pulls out the sandwiches Jo made us.

Once again, the conversation turns to the dance talk in town. Maggie relays who is going with whom, and who is still looking for a date. I don't hear much of it. I just enjoy watching her talk. Every now and then, I nod and take her in. Her smile and how animated she is makes me glad I brought her here.

Her warm voice and slight southern accent washes over me. I love just sitting and talking with her. She could be reading an instruction manual, and she'd still captivate me.

As we finish up lunch, I know I should help her pack everything up, but watching her bending over the blanket and cleaning up, I can't move. Her ass in those jeans is a sight to see.

Before I know it, I'm behind her with my hand on her hips. She stands up putting her back to my chest, and I let my breath warm her ear for just a moment before I talk.

"Do you know what you do to me, sweetheart? You are the most beautiful person I've ever had the privilege of laying eyes on. But you in those jeans? I understand now why your parents didn't want you girls wearing jeans growing up. I'm glad they didn't, because who knows who would have snapped you up before me." I whisper into her ear.

My hands trail down her hips and back to her ass, where I fill my hands with the lush globes and squeeze, causing her to moan. Her sounds make me want to take her right there.

"Let's get back on the horses, I still have the creek to show you, before we head home," I say, as I take a step back.

I know the distance as we ride will do us both a bit of good. I point out different areas, pastures, and trails, as we make our way to the creek. When we hear the water running over the rocks, her smile widens.

"Wow, this is bigger than I expected. Can you fish here?" She asks.

"Yes. When I wade out, the water will be between my waist and my chest, depending on the amount of rain we've had. It's one of my favorite spots in the summer."

"I can see why. I love that it's on the property, our own private swimming hole. I can see lazy summer days here."

As we turn to head home, she keeps talking to me. At one point, she turns to look at me and misses the branch in the path.

It all happens in slow motion. I reach for her, trying to warn her, but there isn't enough time. Her head turns slowly forward, but not fast enough. Her eyes go wide just as the tree branch hits her right across the forehead.

Her body falls backward and slowly slides down the horse's leg to the ground. The horse spooks only a bit and runs ahead a few hundred yards, before stopping to turn back.

I'm down from my horse faster than I thought possible and on the ground by her side.

A million thoughts run through my head. We are away from the house, and if she is really hurt, what's the best way to get her back? Do I have cell service? Are my parents' home to come help?

I fall to my knees in the dirt beside her.

"Maggie, sweetheart." My voice comes out surprisingly steady for how fast my heart is racing.

I start running my hands all over her, looking for any other injuries than a cut on her forehead, and fortunately, I don't find any.

Rubbing my hands along the side of her face, not moving her but wanting to get her attention, I say gently, "Maggie, baby, I need you to wake up for me. I need to see those beautiful eyes and know you're okay." I lean down to place a chaste kiss on her mouth.

As I pull back, she starts to groan, and I breathe a sigh of relief.

"Don't try to move, Maggie, just sit still. You're safe but just relax for me."

She finally opens her eyes, and they lock on me.

"My head and my back hurt."

"Yes, you hit a branch and fell off your horse. Stay there let me grab the first aid kit."

Living on a ranch of any size, you never go out on a horse ride without a first aid kit. My dad taught me that, and it's come in handy more times than I can count.

"How are you feeling? Think you can sit up?" I ask her.

"Yeah." She says, and I help her up to rest against the tree trunk. I gently clean the scratch on her forehead that has already stopped bleeding, and then place a Band-Aid over it to keep it covered on the way home.

I give her some water, as I head over and get her horse.

"Come on, you'll ride with me to be safe."

I help her up on my horse, and then tie her horse's reins to my saddle and climb on behind her.

Chapter 18

Maggie

Nick has been a perfect gentleman since we got back to the house. I could tell my fall shook him as much as it did me, but he's been making sure I'm taken care of.

We got back to the house, and he finished up dinner. He insisted I sit and relax, so I got to watch him, while he was in the kitchen, in his element, and that's a sight I won't soon forget.

He pulled me onto his lap at dinner and fed me every bite. This might annoy some people, but I loved being so close to him, and I didn't mind. Plus, I could tell it soothed him to take care of me.

Now, we are sitting on the back porch, and I'm watching him build a fire in the fire pit, and cowboy Nick is just as sexy as chef Nick.

His movements are sure and steady. His muscles ripple, as he lifts the firewood and moves to light the fire.

In no time flat, the fire is roaring to life, and I can already feel the heat of it. Nick disappears inside for a few minutes and comes back out with a blanket over one arm and a tray full of everything needed to make s'mores.

"No more putting off calling your parents," Nick tells me. He's been insisting I tell them about the fall and let them know I'm staying at his place to be safe. I've been avoiding it because I haven't actually had the talk about staying at his place at all.

So, I chicken out and call Ella instead.

"Hey, Mags!" Ella answers the phone.

"Hey, El. I need a favor."

Nick's eyes turn to me, and he shakes his head with a ghost of a smile on his lips. He knows what I'm doing, and it looks like he will let me slide this time.

"Of course, what's up?" Ella asks.

"Listen, I'm at Nick's, and we were out riding horses earlier today, and I fell and hit my head. I'm fine!" I get out just before Ella freaks.

"Maggie, are you okay?" Her high pitched voice comes over the line. The one she uses, when she's truly concerned about someone. I can picture Jason instantly by her side to step in if needed.

"I'm fine, I swear. It's just Nick doesn't want me driving, so I'm going to stay here tonight but..." I trail off not sure if it's fair to ask her to talk to Mom and Dad for me.

But Ella has always been able to read my thoughts.

"But you need me to tell Mom and Dad because they don't know how serious you and Nick are."

"Yes, please."

"Of course, Maggie. You let us know if you need anything, okay?"

"Promise."

"Love you, Mags."

"Love you too, El."

I hang up the phone and look up at Nick, who hasn't taken his eyes off me.

"Sneaky, sneaky, but I'll let it slide."

"I'll have to talk to my parents about us soon, but I don't want to do it tonight."

"I'm only going to let it slide because you hurt yourself today, and I just want to cuddle." He says as he pulls me from my chair into his lap.

I snuggle into him, as he covers us with a blanket, and he starts making s'mores. There's something very comforting in watching the simple task of him making a s'more; sliding the marshmallow on to the stick and roasting it on the fire until it's just right. In my case, that means, until the outside is nice and burnt.

Then, the smashing of the hot, gooey marshmallow between the chocolate and graham crackers.

Is it normal to get turned on watching him make the perfect s'more? It can't be just me.

As he holds the delicacy up to my lips, I lock eyes with him and take my first bite. Now, there's just no way to gracefully eat it. It's messy, sticky, and yummy. I think about taking a small bit to minimize the mess but come on. These are s'mores, and there are no small bites when it comes to them.

Of course, there's some sticky marshmallow on the corner of my mouth. I bring my hand up to clean it, but Nick stops me. He sets the s'mores down on the tray, angles my head, and slowly licks it off. His mouth moves from the corner of mine on to my lips.

His kiss is soft and slow, enough to tease, but not enough to give either of us what we want or need. I can feel his cock getting hard against my hips, but when I try to deepen the kiss, he pulls back. He smiles against my lips, as he keeps the soft kisses going.

I'm in such a haze from his kiss, I don't hear anything around us. So, when he pulls away, I let out a little moan.

"I'm sorry, sweetheart. I didn't know they were coming over tonight." He whispers in my ear.

I'm about to ask him what he means when a woman's voice fills the air.

"Oh, honey, I wish you had told me you were lighting a fire I could have brought some hot chocolate." A moment later, an older woman steps through the door on the back porch and stops in her tracks, when she sees me.

"Oh, Nick! You should have told us Maggie was coming over! Bill, did he tell you Maggie was going to be here?" She turns to her husband, who walks up behind her.

"No, dear, I would have told you." He smiles and then turns to me. "But I'm sure glad to meet you. I'm Bill, and this is my wife, Laura. We're Nick's parents."

I try to stand up to greet them, but Nick tightens his grip on me and lets out a little growl, causing his parents to laugh.

"Well, it's nice to meet you, too. Why don't you join us?" I offer.

"Oh no, we won't intrude." Laura waves me off.

"Please, I want to get to know you. I wasn't planning on being here tonight anyway, but gravity and I didn't get along today." I try to joke.

Laura's face goes stone cold. "What happened?"

"My mom's a nurse, so you just kicked in her medical training side, be warned," Nick whispers in my ear.

"We were riding, and a branch hit her on the forehead and knocked her off the horse. I didn't want her driving, so I convinced her to stay here. I promise, I did everything you taught me to, and she's fine."

"Posh." Laura waves her hand at him. "Maggie, dear, why don't you come inside and let me take a look just to calm my momma nerves."

"Okay." This time Nick lets me stand up, and I pass Bill, who pats my shoulder.

"Just give in to her, it's easier than fighting." He says, and he takes the chair next to Nick.

I follow Laura into the dining room, where she has me sit down and checks my eyes, and asks me a bunch of questions. Many of them I recognize from the time I was with Royce in the emergency room when he crashed his bike when we were kids.

Then, she removes the bandage from my forehead and checks the cut. I still haven't seen it myself, so I will take her word on it.

"Nick cleaned it up right away. He had a first aid kit he brought with us," I tell her.

"I taught my son well, but a mother will always worry." She says, and then goes down the hall and comes back with a basket she sets on the table and starts rummaging through it.

"Don't I know it? I chickened out and had called my sister and told her what happened and had her tell my mom. I know she'll pounce as soon as I walk in the door tomorrow. My sister is good at keeping them calm."

"It's a mother's right to worry. No matter how old our kids get, we never stop worrying. I'm going to clean it again, put some cream on it, and bandage it, so we can minimize the scarring. Tomorrow, you can take the bandage off and let it heal in some fresh air."

She gets to work, and before I know it, she is done.

"Why don't you head back out there, and I'll make us all some hot chocolate?" She says.

I agree and go back out to the porch. Nick and his dad are talking about spring plans on the ranch, so I try to sit down next to Nick and not interrupt them.

"Not a chance, sweetheart." Nick stops mid conversation, pulling me back onto his lap and under the blanket."

Nick's dad chuckles, but then keeps going with the conversation, like nothing happened.

When Nick's mom brings out the hot chocolate, the conversation shifts to me.

"So, your family recently moved to Rock Springs?" His mom asks.

"Yes, my sister married Jason, and my brother has been trying to get Anna Mae to give him the time of day. It was at a good point to move, and Mom and Dad want to be around the grandkids that will come someday. I loved the ranch, and I want to be near my sister, so I followed."

"Oh, don't sugar coat it. We know what that bastard Seth did to your sister, and how the church back home treated your family," Laura says.

To say I'm a bit shocked is an understatement. It must show on my face because she answers my unspoken question.

"We've had lunch with Jason and Ella, and they told us. We're glad you are here by the way. Never seen my Nick so happy."

"Nick says you are a photographer?" His dad asks.

"Yeah, I actually have a photoshoot at the diner next week. Jo wants to re-do her menus and website, so I'm taking photos of the food and the place."

"We should have some done of the ranch and update our website," Bill says.

Nick and his dad start talking about good places to get pictures, and how to update the website, but I hear none of it. I can't concentrate on anything other than Nick's hand on my thigh, and his thumb rubbing small soft circles over my jeans.

Even with the jeans between us, I can feel every movement, and it's very distracting. It's also very calming. I rest my head on Nick's shoulder and relax. I guess I drift off because the next thing I hear is Nick's mom.

"Poor thing has had such a long day. We're going to get going. You get her to bed, but make sure you check on her throughout the night. I didn't see any signs of a concussion, but we can't be too careful. Then, you call me, if there are any problems. I can be right over." Laura says, and I open my eyes just in time to see her lean over and give Nick a kiss on his forehead.

"I will, Mom. Thank you." His dad shakes his hand and turns to put out the fire before they head back into the house and out the front door.

"Let's get you to bed, sweetheart," Nick says, as he shifts and stands up with me in his arms.

"I didn't mean to fall asleep. I was just so relaxed and warm, snuggling with you." I say around a yawn.

"It's okay. I'm glad you're relaxed. Let's get you ready for bed. I'll wake you up a few times to check on you throughout the night, okay?"

"Okay," I sigh.

He helps me out of my jeans and into one of his shirts, before tucking me into bed. I curl up next to him, and he wraps his arms around me, holding me tight.

Chapter 19

Maggie

I'm packing up my camera bag and working off some different photo ideas in my head for this shoot at the diner today. The last week with Nick started off great, but the last few days, he seems to be pulling away.

The dance is right around the corner, and I know he's busy, as are Jason and Ella, so I'm trying not to let my mind wander to that dark corner and make myself worry over nothing.

Even Ella said Nick has been working late hours, getting ready for the dance. He wants to prove to Jason he can do more than just the kitchen side. I know that and keep reminding myself that he's busy for now, but it will slow down soon.

So today, I'm going to busy myself with this photoshoot, and then head over to see Nick afterward, even if it's just for a few minutes.

I double check that I have everything, including a few extra memory cards, and then leave.

"Maggie, if you aren't coming home tonight, then YOU need to call us, okay?"

My mom has said this to me every time I walk out of the house, since that night at Nick's.

As I expected, she was waiting for me the next morning and wanted details. She agreed that I shouldn't have driven, but she said her and dad could have come to pick me up, instead of inconveniencing Nick. When I said it wasn't an inconvenience for me to stay there, I know she understood more than I meant to say.

That night Mom and Dad sat me down and gave me the safe sex speech yet again, but in more detail than they did when Ella and I were kids. Mom asked if I wanted her to take me to get on the pill, and Daddy said I should never feel forced, and no matter what time or the reason I could call him to come pick me up, no questions asked.

It did make me want to slow things down with Nick. I explained the conversation, and it wasn't long after that he started to pull away. Ella swears it's just a coincidence, but the dark side of my brain isn't so sure.

I try to push this all from my head on the drive into town. I jam out to some country music and try to keep things upbeat. The last thing I need is for the Rock Springs gossip vultures to suspect something is wrong and start to dig. They are ruthless with their lines of questions when they have a bone.

I park around the back of the building and head across the street to get some photos of the front of the building. The diner has a very nostalgic feel. Jo has done a great job keeping it updated, but still retaining the vintage feel the town loves.

I found some old photos from the 1950s with old cars in front of the diner, so I make sure I get a few photos from the same angle, so we can put them side by side for comparisons. I get a few photos with people in them and some without, before going inside.

Once in the diner, I take a few candid pictures of some of the ranchers at the counter drinking coffee. It captures the feel of Rock Springs perfectly with them in their flannel shirts and cowboy hats.

"Maggie! I'm so excited you're here." Jo greets me with a huge hug. "Tell me what you need."

"Oh, I just need a place to set my stuff up. A small corner out of the way will work perfectly."

Jo leads me to a small corner table, and I set my stuff down.

"Do you want to see some of the outside shots I got?" I ask her.

"Of course!" She says with her bubbly excitement.

I show her the photos and the vintage photo comparisons.

"Oh, I love that idea! We can print both and hang them side by side on the walls!" She looks around the diner.

The front of the dinner is all windows, looking out over Main Street, but the sides have some wall space decorated with memorabilia from around town, like license plates, horseshoes, and old signs.

"Okay, I have a few desserts I thought we could start with, while we cook up some other food."

We spend the next several hours with her bringing me food and helping me style it. We use the counter with the diner in the background blurred out for food shots. Jo has a good eye for food styling and seems to be enjoying our time together.

"Okay, break time. I insist you eat!" Jo brings me out a turkey club with her herbed mayo that I love.

She sits and talks with me, while I eat.

"You're going to the dance with Nick, right?"

"Yeah, I'm excited. It's his first time going to the dance as a guest. He normally works it."

A knowing look crosses her face. I know she's thinking of the Sweetheart's Dance legend that everyone has been talking about. What I don't admit is that I hope it's true.

"He's been really busy lately getting ready for the dance, but I did meet his parents. By accident, but it still counts."

"It sure does!" Her smile fades, as the bell rings, letting everyone know someone just walked in the door.

"Well, we got another city girl who must be in Rock Springs shopping for the day."

I turn to look and see it's Lauren. Her clothes and designer sunglasses scream city girl.

"You have got to be kidding me," I mumble, but it's enough to stop Jo in her tracks.

"You know her?" She asks.

I give her the short version of how we met and her last visit here. At the reminder, Jo recognizes her.

"So, she's here and up to no good." Jo frowns.

We both watch the waitress serve her a coffee before she turns and looks around. The moment her eyes land on me, everyone knows it. Her smirk confirms Jo's statement. Whatever she has to say won't be good.

She takes her time, walking over to the table, and then sitting in the empty chair next to me.

"Where's Nick at?" She asks smugly.

"He's getting ready for the dance. I'm meeting up with him later after I'm done with my work here," I say.

"What are you, a waitress now?" She somehow makes the word waitress sound dirty.

"No, she's a kick-ass photographer, who's taking photos for my new menus and my website." Jo chimes in, and I can tell by her tone that her protective side is coming out.

Lauren nods her head and just looks at us, so I ask the obvious question.

"What are you doing out this way?" I'm not sure I even want to know the answer.

"Well, Nick mentioned the dance last time I was here, and I wanted to come out and see how it's going, and to check if he's doing any new food items for the event."

I want to know if Nick invited her out, but I won't be that girl, and I won't give her the satisfaction. Thankfully, Jo seems to read my mind.

"Does he know you're coming?" Jo asks.

"No, I thought I'd surprise him. I'm sure he needs a break from all the planning, or maybe, he needs some help. He's a chef, not an event planner."

"You know, he's busy, and I'm not sure he'll have time for you. Besides, my sister and I are helping with a lot of the planning." My catty side that I never knew I had pops out. I don't know who this girl is, and I don't recognize her, but all I feel is this need to protect Nick. He can do anything he puts his mind to, and who the hell is she to suggest otherwise?

"Well, I guess we'll see. Have fun taking your photos." With that, she stands up and walks out of the diner.

It's then I realize everyone has stopped what they were doing to watch us. I try to offer them a smile with more confidence than I feel.

"You look like you need a shot of whiskey," Jo says to me.

"I feel like it, too. Too bad you don't have any of that here."

"No, but I know a place across the street, where you can get it."

I know she's suggesting I go to WJ's behind Lauren.

"I trust Nick. Let me finish up here. I only have a few more shots, then I'll pack up and head over."

It takes less time than I thought to take the last shots I needed, so I take my time, putting my equipment away. If I'm being honest, I'm stalling, because I'm really hoping Lauren will be gone, before I get there. I know my Nick, and he will kick her out the first chance he gets.

I load everything into my truck and make the short drive over to WJ's parking lot.

Taking several calming breaths, I walk into the bar to go see Nick.

As I walk in the door, my hopes that Lauren is gone, are dashed, because I hear her voice talking about the dance. I just don't see her or Nick, until I get closer to the bar.

Her arms are wrapped around his neck, and they're kissing. My eyes are only on them for a split second, but the image is seared into my brain in high definition detail.

I don't even care what the excuse or reasoning is. I just turn and run out of the door to my truck. I'm in such a hurry to get out of the parking lot that I don't even buckle my seat belt. My mind starts racing on where to go. Somewhere he won't go to look for me, because the ranch will be his first stop.

I point my truck out of town and hit the gas.

Chapter 20

Nick

The week before the dance I had no idea there was so much that needed to be done. Deliveries to be scheduled, since everyone wants to verify the time and their orders, placing the restaurant's food and bar orders, making sure we have all the decorations, confirming the band and going over the band's playlist, and making sure we have extra security. The list goes on and on, and that's on top of my normal day-to-day duties around WJ's.

Every time I make plans with Maggie, something comes up. I've canceled on her twice. When we do talk, it's as if I'm on my way home. Once, I fell asleep on the phone with her, because I'd laid down. That night I didn't even get my boots off.

Today, I know she's doing a photo shoot at the diner with Jo, and then she's coming over and hanging out. I'd rather have her here, when I make phone calls than not see her at all, and she feels the same.

I've told her how much pulling this dance off means to me. I want to prove to Jason he made the right choice in making me a partner. I want him to know how grateful I am. Maggie understands, and she has been helping in any way she can. She made sure we sold every last ticket to the dance and has been working with Ella on the decorations. Seeing her take an interest in what is important to me, makes me proud to call this girl mine.

I finish up my lunch and debate on texting her, but I don't want to bother her during the shoot, because I know how excited she was for it. Just a few more hours, and she will be here in my arms, I remind myself.

I'm doing inventory on the bar when the door opens. My heart races knowing Maggie is here. I finish the shelf I'm working on, and when I turn around, my heart drops. It's not Maggie, but Lauren.

"Hey there, cowboy." She says in what I'm sure she thinks is her sexy voice, but to me, it's like nails on a chalkboard.

I turn back to the bar and continue my inventory.

"What do you want?" I try to be polite, but I'm sure it doesn't come out that way.

"Now, is that any way to greet a girl who just drove all the way from Dallas to see you?" She takes a step closer to me, trying to box me into the bar. Thankfully, the bar lifts on the other side for an easy exit if needed.

"It's how I greet someone I don't want to be around." This time I don't hide the anger in my voice.

Her face falls just a bit before she recovers and tries again.

"Come on, Nick. We'd be good together, and we'd be able to push each other. Hell, we could team up and have the best restaurants in Dallas, or heck, even in the state."

At one time, that was the dream, and I'd have jumped at any way to get there. But I had the big city fancy restaurant life, and I don't want it again.

"I know this might be hard for you to understand, but that isn't my dream. I'm right where I want to be. Right here in Rock Springs with my friends and family and my girl."

She scoffs, and I ignore her attempting to get the inventory done.

"Seriously, Nick. No one becomes a chef and wins a championship just to settle down in some Podunk small-town."

I stand and turn to face her. "I did. Now leave."

I try to move past her, but she gets in my way. I hear the door open again, and before I can turn to see who it is, Lauren catches me off guard, pulling me into a kiss. Not a millisecond after her lips touch mine, I hear a gasp behind me.

I push Lauren away and see Maggie, running out of the door.

Damn it.

"Well, that's one less thing holding you here." She says with a sick smirk on her face. I shoot up a silent prayer that God and my mama will forgive me for raising my voice to a female for the first time, since grade school.

"Get out!" I yell louder than I have ever raised my voice in my life. "Get the hell out and don't you dare set foot back on this property again, or I'll have you arrested for harassment and trespassing."

It's then, Jason steps out of the office and looks between us.

"Jason, make sure she leaves. I have to go after Maggie. Call Ella, Maggie is going to need someone to talk to, because I'm sure she won't want to talk to me again."

I look once more at Lauren, who looks purely shocked. "There's no way I would ever want to be with a girl like you. You are so ugly inside that I can't stand to be around you." Then, I turn and run after Maggie.

As I get to the door, I find Maggie's truck, pulling out of the parking lot. Watching her truck roll down Main Street, feels like she's pulling my heart with her. I have the kind of love for her that means I can't live without her. Right now, she's hurt, and the thought that it was me who hurt her is more than I can take. The bar door opens and closes behind me, and a moment later Jason is beside me, as a truck I'm assuming is Lauren's, pulls out and heads towards the interstate, and the opposite way as Maggie.

"What happened? I have Ella on speakerphone," Jason says.

I kick at a rock. "Damn it!" I take a deep breath and prepare to explain. I'm going to need Ella's help, if I'm going to pull this off, before the dance in a few days.

"Maggie was supposed to come to the bar, when she was finished with her shoot with Jo. Well, Lauren showed up before her and was saying all this stuff about working together and me getting out of Rock Springs. I turned her down and told her to leave, and as I tried to walk by her, she kissed me. I pushed her away the second it happened, but Maggie saw, and by the time I turned to her, she was running out of the door. I never got to talk to her. My guess is she's heading to the ranch. If you can talk to her Ella, be there for her. I'm going to fix this, I swear it."

"Kelli did that to Colt here at WJ's, and Sage saw. You can talk to them, if you need help," Jason says.

"Please, just make sure she's okay," I beg.

"Hang on, I got a text from her," Ella says.

"Well, she isn't coming to the ranch, but I won't tell you where she is, because she wants to be alone for a while. Get a plan in the works and don't let her go to bed tonight without at least explaining what happened."

"Thank you, Ella. Are your parents' home?" I ask.

"Yes, I believe so. I was down there an hour ago, and they were there."

Jason hangs up with Ella and turns to me.

"What's your plan?" He asks.

"I'm not 100% sure. I know I'm going to marry her, even if it takes me years to earn her trust back. I'm going to start by getting her parents' blessing."

I run towards my truck and climb in. If Maggie isn't heading back to the ranch, I'm not sure where she's going, but it also means I can talk to her parents alone, before I make my move. If I'm lucky, they might even have a few ideas for me.

I don't even make it a block, before I whip into a parking spot in front of a shop on Main Street. Maggie was telling me about a vintage camera she saw here last week.

"Hey, Nick!" The shopkeeper says.

"Hey, Maggie was in here last week and was telling me about a vintage camera you had. Do you still have it by chance?"

"Oh yes, right back here." She shows me an old camera with a crank. "This is a 1931

Rolleiflex. It still works, and there's a camera shop in Dallas that sells the film for it. The gentleman is very knowledgeable and would be happy to give a lesson on how to use it as well."

"Perfect, I'll take it. Also, if you can write down the shop's info for me."

"Oh, Maggie is going to be so tickled! She spent an hour in here, looking at the camera and looking up information on it."

One of the disadvantages of Rock Springs is everyone takes their time. Normally, I love this, but right now, every second feels like an hour going by. Maggie is slipping further and further away, and I'm just trying to keep it together.

After she wraps the camera up and I pay for it, I settle the camera on the passenger's floor and make sure it's nice and secure, before climbing back in and driving towards Jason's family ranch.

I send up a silent prayer that Maggie's parents are home, and that they will even talk to me. For all I know, Maggie has called them, and they are angry at me on their daughter's behalf, and they have every right.

As I make the twenty-minute drive out of town, I rehearse what I want to say to them over and over, but the moment I pull into the ranch, all the words escape me.

This is one of the most important things I will ever do. Making things right with my future wife's parents. Proving to them I can take care of her, and that I'm the right person to give their daughter to.

For a brief moment, a little girl with Maggie's smile flashes in my mind, and the thought of handing my daughter over to even the perfect guy is something I don't know how I will be able to do.

I park my truck in front of Maggie's parents' place and take my time getting out. I slowly make my way up the front porch and knock on the door.

"Nick! Ella told us you were on your way over to talk with us. You're just in time for dinner. Please, tell me you'll join us?" Maria, Maggie's mom, greets me with a hug.

"Of course, I will. There's nothing that could stop me from a home cooked meal of yours." I'm not just blowing smoke up her ass either. Her food is some of the best in town, and she could give me a run for my money. "Have you talked to Maggie?"

"Not since she left for the diner this morning. Is everything okay?" Grant, her father, asks.

"There might have been an incident, and me being here is the first step to making it right. Let's sit down, and I'll explain everything."

I start with me doing inventory, and tell them about Lauren walking in, and what she said. The kiss and how Maggie saw it, and the call with Ella. I don't leave a detail out. They let me finish, and when I'm done, Grant sits back and gives me his patient dad stare. I know he's taking in everything I said.

"I guess telling us the whole story isn't why you're here." He says when he finally speaks.

"No, sir. I'm here to ask your permission to marry your daughter. I know it's going to take some groveling to win her back and earn her trust again, but I'm ready to do it. But when the time comes, I want to know I have your support."

"And just how do you plan to win her back?" Maria asks.

"Lots of groveling and begging. I'm not stopping. I deserve whatever she throws at me. I plan to start by telling her the truth about what happened. I know it won't make it hurt any less, but I have to start somewhere."

"Did you make it clear with this Lauren that she needs to leave you alone?" Grant asks.

"Yes, in fact, it was the first time I raised my voice to a female, since I was a kid. She looked ready to cry at one point, and I didn't even feel sorry. That might make me a bad person, but I didn't want there to ever be any doubt I meant what I said. I also threatened to have her arrested, if she showed back up. I'm not sure I'd have grounds to do it other than she has been banned from WJ's, but I'll sure as hell try."

Grant and Maria seem to have a silent conversation between them before Grant stands up. I do the same, as he walks over to me and holds out his hand.

"It would be an honor to have you as a son-in-law. I know how happy you make Maggie, and I know she loves you. Make this right, sooner rather than later."

"I will, sir. I promise."

Both Grant and Maria hug me, and I head home with a huge smile on my face. Next, is to tell Maggie the truth of what happened, and I plan to do that via text, so she can read it, but she doesn't have to answer. I know Ella is with her, so I can send it to Ella too and ask her to make sure she reads it.

My plan starts to click into place, and I send up a prayer it will be enough.

Chapter 21

Maggie

Knowing I can't go home, because that is the first place Nick will look, has my mind racing. Then, I see Hunter's truck at the vet clinic, and a light bulb goes off. I take the turn, leading towards his parents' house and Mike and Lilly's next door.

I've been meaning to check out the pregnant horse anyway and see how she's doing. I know Snow White is back on her feet and doing well. I also know everyone is still a little nervous about her unborn horse because they aren't sure what lasting effects the drugs in her system will have.

My phone goes off, but I ignore it until I pull into Lilly and Mike's place and park my truck. I almost turn my phone off without looking, but then, I see it's my sister, Ella. I know she will worry, so I shoot her a quick call.

"Hey, I heard from Jason what happened. Tell me you're safe."

"I'm safe. I just pulled into Lilly's, but if you tell anyone, I'll murder you in your sleep." I wish I was joking, but right now, I can't say that I am.

"Sister code takes first place here," she says. "Mags, I know you're mad, but promise me you will at least listen to what he has to say when he talks to you. Just hear him out, you don't even have to talk to him."

"Fine," I grit out between my teeth.

"I love you, Mags. Let me know if you need anything."

"I love you too, and I will."

We hang up, and I take a deep breath and walk up to the house. Lilly is already waiting for me on the front porch. Rock Springs gossip travels fast. Really, really, really fast, because Lilly has already heard what happened, at least, some version of it, and just hugs me.

"Mike is making tacos." She says as we walk in the door, and the most tantalizing food smell hits me.

"Be happy you already married him, or I'd ask him to marry me on the spot." I try to joke, but there isn't much amusement in it.

"How about I call the girls, and we have a girls' night? I can mix up some margaritas, and Mike can make some more tacos and salsa?"

"Sounds good." I sigh, as I plop down on her couch.

Lilly sends out a group text, and I lie down on the couch and try not to cry. I run the whole day over in my head and exhaustion hits me.

The next thing I know, the girls are walking in the house. I guess I fell asleep. Ella runs right over to me and wraps me in her arms, which just reminds me of home. Riley, Sarah, Sage, and Megan aren't far behind her.

When Ella married into this family, it's like I did, too. They accepted me with open arms, and on nights like tonight, it's very much needed.

"Okay, food is on the counter, and Lilly has the drinks under control. Hunter invited me over to his parents' place for some cards, so I'll be just next door if you need me." Mike says, kissing Lilly on the cheek and walking out of the door.

We all pile our plates high with food and get comfortable in the living room.

"Alright, we want to know the story. I'm sure we have all heard one version or other, and who knows how much truth is behind them," Riley says.

I recap my whole day from the photo shoot to running into Lauren at the diner and then heading into WJ's to find them kissing.

"Now, don't kill me on this," Sage starts. "But this sounds a lot like what Kelli did to me."

"That was before our time," Ella says.

"Mine, too," Sarah adds.

"Well, I had been in Tennessee helping Abby, after her parents died. It took longer than we thought to get everything wrapped up. So, I decided to surprise Colt and stop into WJ's that night. I hadn't told him I was coming home. Jason had asked him to work more to keep him busy than anything else."

She takes a big sip of her margarita.

"So, I walk in, the place was packed, and I didn't see him sitting at a table at first, but Kelli saw me. She sat on Colt's lap and kissed him. Of course, all I see is the kiss. I was crushed. I ran out and right to our cabin. I wanted nothing to do with Colt."

Sage pauses for some more chips and salsa. "Turns out, Kelli saw me and was trying to break us up and cause problems. The second I was out of the door, Colt yelled at her in front of everyone, and made her cry, and then came after me. He explained, Jason explained, and half the town explained. Just hear him out. This Lauren girl seems like just as big a snake as Kelli."

"Hey, but we got our revenge!" Megan says, and Sage and Riley burst out laughing.

"How?" I have to know because revenge sounds pretty good right now. Though right now, I'm feeling a bit buzzed, too.

"We arranged for a morning alarm service to wake her up with an air horn in her ear every morning for two months. If she didn't answer, it kept calling back, until she did, and every day, it was a new phone number." Sage laughs.

"That's so evil!" Sarah says, but we all laugh.

"It was all Megan's idea." Riley points to Megan across the room, who grins and takes a stage bow from her seat.

"Remind us never to get on your bad side." Lilly jokes though it's the truth.

"Kelli had it coming for years. All the crap she pulled with Sage and Colt, and even on some of the other guys."

"Her and Cindy are friends. Cindy ditched me one day in high school, and it led to me finding Hunter. That's the good part, but she isn't too nice to anyone else either," Megan says.

The girls all talk about the bumps in the road they had before they got married. It's good to know I'm not the only one with a rocky road, and it makes me think I might have a chance to work this out. *Maybe.*

Just as I'm thinking this, a text comes in from Nick, and it's a long one. I'm debating reading it when Ella's phone goes off.

"I'm supposed to make sure you read that text. You don't have to answer or say a word, but you should read it." Ella says, and Lilly makes me another margarita.

Nick: Maggie, I know you are hurting right now, and that kills me. I need you to read this, even if nothing comes of it. I just need you to know the truth. I had heard you come into WJ's and ended the conversation with Lauren and was trying to walk by her since she had me cornered in the bar. Before I could move by, she pulled me in for a kiss. I pushed her away instantly, and by the time I turned, you were already backing out of the door. Then, I did something I promised my dad I would never do. I raised my voice to a female. I was so loud Jason came out of the office. I told Lauren to leave and not come back. I banned her from WJ's and told her, if she steps foot in there again, I'll call the cops and file harassment charges. I think she left crying, and I hope she did. That might make me a bastard, but the thought of you crying rips my heart out. I heard she was at the diner, before she came into WJ's, and thinking she planned all this, well, I wish I had made her cry more. I'll be here waiting for you Mags, until my last breath. You are it for me, and I know it. Call any time, day or night, and I will always answer. - Nick

I didn't realize I had started to cry until Lilly hands me a tissue. Squaring my shoulders, thinking of a way to change the subject, I'm relieved when I hear a horse from the barn.

"Can we go check on Snow White?" I ask.

A huge smile crosses Lilly's face. "Of course, horses always make everything better," Lilly says.

We all bundle up in our boots and jackets and head on down to the barn. It's now when you can tell who has had more to drink than the others.

Megan who is sober, because she's pregnant, is trying to hold up Riley and Sage, who are both having trouble walking a straight line.

Sarah is walking behind them and tripping over her own two feet, which makes Lilly laugh so hard she almost trips over herself. Ella and I bring up the rear, arms locked together.

"I don't think I ever thanked you for this," I say to her.

"For what?" She asks.

"For this family. You were brave and took a chance on Jason, breaking some of Mom and Dad's rules, and in doing so, you gave me a large family, and some of the best friends I've ever had." I say.

"Maggie, that's the margaritas talking. You're hard not to love. All your life people have gravitated towards you, and you always made sure I was included, so I'm happy to return the favor."

"That's what big sisters do." I sigh, as we reach the barn.

"What horse is this one?" I ask, looking at the black horse in the first stall.

"That's Black Diamond. He was the first one left at the church parking lot. Even though he warmed up to people a bit, he still can spook pretty easy."

We walk down to Snow White's stall and find her on the ground.

"Shit, she's in labor. Megan call Hunter. I know the guys are next door."

We all seem to sober up pretty fast, as Megan runs out of the door to make the call, and Lilly heads into the stockroom and starts pulling down supplies.

"Here, Maggie, will you help me carry these?" Lilly says, handing me some blankets and a pair of really long gloves. We get back to the stall, as the guys come running into the barn. Hunter and Mike are first, followed by Blaze, Colt, Jason, and Mac. Hunter's dad is the last one in, carrying a bag looking a lot like Hunter's, which I'm guessing is his medical bag.

Mike, Hunter, and Hunter's dad, Hank, go into the stall, while the rest of us spread out along the edges to watch. Thankfully, it's a corner cell with a side aisle, so there are two walls we can watch from.

"Look out, she's peeing," Ella giggles.

"No, that's her water leaking," Hunter says, and he and Hank both pull on the long gloves that go up to their shoulders. Mike goes around slowly to the front of Snow and helps keep her calm. They seem to share a special bond, because she calms down, as soon as she sees him.

No sooner does Snow calm than a huge contraction hits and her water breaks in a huge gush of fluid. Hunter and Hank both get it on their boots before they get down to take a look at Snow. Hank starts talking his way through what he's doing. You can tell he's a natural born teacher.

"We want to let her do as much work as she can on her own, and then only intervene if she's in trouble. I'm not sure what to expect with the drugs that were in her system. We've been monitoring the foal, and all looked good, but you just never know," Hank says.

The barn is quiet with the exception of Mike's gentle whispering, and the noises from the horses.

A moment later, two small hoofs appear, and with each push, a little more of the foal's legs are pushed out still in a watery sack.

Another dozen or so pushes, and a small head appears. Snow looks like she's resting, and I wonder if this has stalled the birth process when she starts pushing again. A few large pushes and the head is out, and then the rest of the body just seems to slide out.

We all watch in awe, as the baby horse in front of us kicks its feet just enough to break the film over it and starts breathing. He or she lays there and slowly starts trying to move its neck, as Snow catches her breath.

The new little one is mostly white with a few pinkish spots that I'm sure will change, as he or she grows.

Over the next half hour, we watch mama clean up her new baby, as the foal tries to stand. When the little one finally gets on its feet, we all let out a whispered cheer. It's a girl, Hank says, and Lilly laughs.

"She looks like a peppermint," Lilly says.

Mike locks eyes with her. "That's her name, Peppermint."

We all agree it suits her and watch a bit longer, as Peppermint nurses for the first time.

"Lilly and I will stay in the barn tonight and watch over them," Mike says.

"I'll turn my ringer up. I'm right next door if you need me," Hank says and packs up his stuff. Couples slowly start leaving after taking hundreds of photos to share.

"Want a ride back with us?" Ella asks. "We can come back to get your car tomorrow."

With one last look at Peppermint, I agree and follow Jason and Ella out of the barn.

On the way home, I can't stop thinking about Peppermint and watching a new life come into the world. Just a few hours ago, she wasn't even here; it's a reminder of how precious life is. I made myself a promise a while ago to live it to the fullest.

The next few days are going to be crazy with the preparations for the dance, but I make myself a promise to go talk to Nick the day after the dance.

Chapter 22

Nick

The hardest thing I've ever had to do was let Maggie have her space over the last few days. Ella assured me Maggie read my text, and like I promised, I let her have time to process it all.

Today, is the day of the dance, Valentine's Day, the day of love, and boy do I love Maggie. More than I ever thought possible.

Ella and Jason have been keeping me updated on Maggie. Jason mostly telling me where she was going to be, so I could avoid the area. I didn't want her to think I'm following her. What Jason doesn't know is that I also used that information to catch a few glimpses of her. To see for myself that she was doing okay.

The whole thing backfired anyway. She wasn't smiling and happy, she was sad, and I could tell she hasn't been sleeping very well by the bags under her eyes. The fact that I couldn't pull her into my arms and make everything better really weighed on me.

Today, I'm at WJ's, overseeing the last of the setup and making sure all the vendors have their space, and what they need, and Ella has been texting me. They know my plan for tonight and agreed to help. Ella texted me a picture of Maggie's dress, so I could match the color to my clothes. She has been keeping me up to date on her hair and nail appointment.

I had Ella insist on going to Megan's salon and getting their hair and nails done, and I paid for both of them. I wanted to give Maggie time to relax and be pampered. She deserves it. Ella agreed to keep it a secret that I was the one who paid for it, until after the dance.

I watch my mom, Jason's mom, and several church ladies get the arch into position in the entryway. This is the sacred arch that has spawned every tradition and rumored to be what has caused all the matches in town. Walking under this arch with your date, is said to seal the deal between soul mates.

I'm not sure I believed in all that until now, but I'm not taking any chances. I always walked around the arch, when working parties, and I have yet to walk under it. Tonight, will be my first night doing so. Each year, the church ladies spruce the arch up and make it look more modern. This year they have added some balloons and lots of twinkle lights.

Once the arch is in place, I head into the back office to get ready. The dance starts in less than an hour, and Ella promised to let me know when they were on their way, and when they were pulling into the parking lot. As I'm finishing with my tie, a text comes in.

Ella: Leaving the ranch now.

Four simple words. They start my heart racing, and my palms get instantly sweaty. I go over what I have planned to say again, as I finish getting ready and head out to make one more round.

The band has already started warming up, and some early birds are already here. I know Maggie thinks she's coming early with Ella and Jason, because she's running a photo booth, but the plan was for her to come with them, so I knew when she was here to make sure she didn't walk in without me.

I make my rounds and end at the door, and I don't have to wait long for the next text.

Ella: Pulling in now.

I take a deep breath and send up a silent prayer, as I walk out to the parking lot. I spot Jason's truck easily, and then get my first glimpse of Maggie. She doesn't see me right away, so I get the chance to just stare at her, as I make my way across the parking lot.

She's in a deep purple dress that looks like it was molded to her from the waist up. Around her waist is a pink lace belt that matches the color of her dress perfectly. From the waist down, the dress flairs out a bit and is wavy and loose.

The moment she looks up and sees me, her eyes go wide.

"Maggie, you look breathtaking," I say, my voice hoarser than I'd have liked.

Her cheeks have a pink tinge, when she finally gets a glimpse of me.

"You look really good too, Nick." There's a question in her eyes, even if she doesn't voice it, so I answer it for her.

"I asked you to be my date, and for me, that hasn't changed. Believe in the Sweetheart's Dance legend or not, but I couldn't have you walk in under that arch alone. I've never walked in under it, and I was really looking forward to doing so tonight." I pause for just a moment, "With you."

She hesitates a bit, before turning to look at Ella. I hope Ella is giving her an encouraging nod, because I don't take my eyes off of Maggie. I couldn't if I tried, because I don't want to miss her answer.

When her eyes meet mine again, I think she's going to say no, until a small smile crosses her face.

"Okay," she whispers.

I want to jump for joy and sag with relief at the same time. I'm thankful that I'm able to collect myself enough to walk to her side and place her arm in mine. Jason and Ella walk in ahead of us, and just before we walk in the door, I turn to her again, soaking in the moment.

Once the door opens, the music gets louder, and the whole atmosphere changes. There's electricity in the air. Maggie lets out a small gasp, feeling it, too.

Jason and Ella walk under the arch hand in hand with huge smiles on their faces. Now that it's our turn, I want to slow time down, beg it to stop, and let me soak in this moment a bit longer.

Maggie looks up to me with an enormous smile on her face, and my heart races. Her smile is contagious, and I smile right back at her.

With her arm still tucked in mine, we take the first steps towards the arch. Then, time really does seem to stand still. The music from the band, and the noise from the crowd all fade away, as we step under the Sweetheart's Arch. The room crackles with electricity, and we both stop and look above us, where the noise seems to be coming from. Then, we both look at each other. Time stops, and it's just the two of us in this quiet little bubble.

We take another step and pass through the arch, and the time vacuum we were in ends, and all the sounds and lights come rushing back to us.

In the next moment, it's my mom's voice I hear next to us. "You felt it, didn't you? The crackling and like time stood still?"

I nod, unable to voice my thoughts.

"I felt it too when I walked through it with your daddy. The Sweetheart's Arch has matched a new generation."

There's no denying that sparks are flying like crazy now between Maggie and me. Every place she touches me, even the slightest bit, it's like Pop Rocks, popping on my skin. The closer she is to me, the more peaceful I feel, but the further she gets, the more anxious I am.

To take a moment to think, I pull her right onto the dance floor and into my arms. I hold her close, as I spin her around the dance floor.

"You felt that too, right?" She whispers against my ear.

"Yes." Is all I'm able to say, as I collect my thoughts. I know she read the text, but I need to get this out of the way, so we have a chance at enjoying the night without it hanging over our heads.

"I never asked Lauren here," I say.

"I know. Ella and I had a good talk the other night. I wouldn't put it past her to try to break us up, thinking she could win you over. I don't think it's about you. I think it's about bettering her restaurant with your name."

I let that thought tumble around my head a bit. I knew there was a way she wanted to use me. She was very competitive at the competition, and I guess, she didn't take to losing to me as well as I thought she did.

"I'm sorry I ever took you to her place, when we were in Dallas," I tell Maggie. If I had never taken her there, none of this would have happened.

"This is not your fault, Nick," Maggie says like she can read my mind. "I like to think she made us stronger, because I learned a lot about myself in the last few days."

"Like what?" I ask, desperate to keep her talking, because I think I might like where this conversation is going.

"That I'm stronger than I ever thought I was. That my gut instinct was right about Lauren and her intentions once again, and I should trust it. I also learned how much I love you."

I stop dead in my tracks, right there in the center of the dance floor.

"Say it again." I struggle to get the words out.

A big smile crosses her face. "I love you, Nick." She says it almost shyly, like she isn't sure I feel the same way, and I can't have that.

I frame her face in my hands and make sure she's looking at me.

"I love you too, Maggie. With all my heart and soul, I love you."

She throws her arms around my neck, and right there in the middle of the dance floor with most of the town watching, I kiss her.

It's a kiss that reminds us both we are right where we belong. I try to keep the kiss rated PG, while showing her how much I love her, but it spirals out of control quickly, and I pull back, as we both catch our breath.

That's when I know this is the moment, and I don't think I will ever get a better one. I take Maggie's hands in mine and look into her eyes. They are shining back at me, so full of love. I take a deep breath and drop down on one knee, as Maggie gasps, which gets the attention of people around us, causing more gasps, and the bands stop the music. All eyes are on us.

Even with all the pressure, I've never been more sure of anything in my entire life. Out of the corner of my eye, I can see Maggie's parents front and center watching. I pull out the box that's been hiding in my pocket and open it. Inside, is my grandmother's wedding ring set. It's a 1920's stone surrounded by small diamonds, and it glitters from all sides. I loved seeing my grandma wear it as a kid, and I hope to see it on Maggie's finger really soon.

"Maggie, the day you walked in here with Ella is a day I can still remember clearly. You were in a blue dress with leggings and those sandals you liked to wear all the time before you got a good pair of boots. Your hair was up in a messy bun and not a stitch of makeup on. My world stopped spinning. Life was busy, and it wasn't until New Year's, when I made my move. I kissed you at midnight, and you ran off on me." The crowd laughs a bit, and Maggie gives me a watery grin.

"I don't regret it, because it brought us here. It brought me you. Maggie, you're nothing like the girl I thought I'd marry because I didn't know a girl like you existed. I didn't know enough to dream you up. But now that I've met you, I can never let you go. I promise to show you every day how much I love you. I promise to cook you any meal you want and let you be my official taste tester. And I promise to build you a photography studio, so you can live your dream, like I'll be living mine. So, will you do me the incredible honor and be my wife?"

At this point, tears are pouring down her face uncontrollably, and it makes my heart clench. I don't like to see her cry, even if they are good tears.

"Yes!" She says and throws herself around me, before I can even stand up. The crowd cheers, and as I slide the ring on her finger, the band starts up again.

Epilogue

Royce

As the oldest sibling, it's hard to see your two younger sisters get married before you. Don't get me wrong, I'm so happy for them. It just hit me that Anna Mae may never open up to me, and I'm not sure how I will handle that.

I'm having dinner with my parents tonight. My baby sister, Ella, and her husband, Jason, are here. She was the first one to get married, and she's the youngest of us three. Her meeting Jason is what brought us here to Rock Springs and allowed me to meet Anna Mae, so I owe her more than she knows.

My other sister, Maggie, is here too with her fiancé, Nick. They just got engaged last month on Valentine's Day. I owe her too, because that proposal got Anna Mae to dance with me that night, and I feel like she has opened up a bit more since.

"So, we were talking about the bachelor and bachelorette parties and decided we want to do a joint one," Maggie says.

"Oh, honey, I love that idea," Mom gushes.

Judging by the look Maggie and Nick just shared, there's more to it than that.

"Mom," Maggie starts and then stops. "We want to have it in Las Vegas."

Both my parents' faces goes stone cold.

We grew up in a super conservative family. The girls wore skirts and dresses, no pants. They didn't go anywhere without someone with them, and all dates for boys and girls were supervised.

This is how Ella and Jason dated, and they called it courting. Ella's first kiss wasn't until her wedding day. It worked great for them, but Maggie has always been a free spirit. I knew from an early age those strict rules wouldn't work for her.

When we moved to Rock Springs, she started wearing jeans, and when she started dating Nick, she refused a chaperone. She and Ella talk a lot, and I'm pretty sure they have even had sex, before they were engaged. I don't dare ask though, because there are some things a brother doesn't need to know about his sister.

Needless to say, a party in Las Vegas is way out of the scope of anything that would have been acceptable for any of us this time last year. But Maggie has opened a lot of doors, not just for herself, but for me.

It's made me think maybe the old way of courting is holding Anna Mae back. Maybe, I need to go the more common dating route, like Maggie did. I push the thoughts from my head and watch my parents for the first sign that I need to jump in and redirect the conversation. I'm the big brother, and I always protect them.

"What would that entail?" My dad finally asks with no emotion in his voice.

This time it's Nick who speaks. "Well, it's always been a dream of mine, sir, and Maggie and I talked. We'd like to stay in a themed hotel and have the family, mine, yours, and Jason's family, who are like family to me, with us. We'd do some shows. Take in the tourist sites, rides, and maybe, a little gambling for those who want, too. They have some of the best food buffets there, so we'd check those out, too. I'd like to do a Hoover Dam tour, and maybe, a Grand Canyon tour. No strippers or any of the stuff you think of with a bachelor party. I want it to be something your family would feel comfortable attending."

Mom and Dad look at each other and have a silent conversation I'm all too familiar with before they turn back to Nick and Maggie.

"Okay, but we'll be watching. Don't drag my little girl down a bad path, or I will revoke my blessing." Dad gives Nick a stern look, but he takes it in stride.

"I promise, sir."

Maggie turns to me, "You're coming right, Royce?"

"Depends if I can bring a guest."

"You can bring two because I think you'll have an easier time convincing Mrs. Willow to go to Vegas than you will Anna Mae."

Mrs. Willow is Anna Mae's grandma, and that's who she's been living with, since her divorce. Mrs. Willow is a hoot and a half, and Maggie is right, she will jump at the chance to go. I guess I should talk to her first and get her on my side to convince Anna Mae to come, too.

The next day I head right to the hair salon, because Ella's sister-in-law, Megan, who owns the hair salon, confirms Mrs. Willow will be there this morning. I know Anna Mae will be working too, so I decided to ask Mrs. Willow to lunch with me.

The moment I walk into the beauty salon, all the ladies start fussing over me. The beauty salon is gossip central, and the place to be and be seen for the church ladies of Rock Springs. It's part of why Megan loves the place. Everyone talks and she gets the scoop, before anyone else.

It looks like Mrs. Willow is almost done, so I timed this perfectly, thanks to Megan.

I walk over to Anna Mae's chair and smile. "Hey, beautiful. How are you today?"

She rolls her eyes but smiles back. "I'm good. Need a haircut?"

"Actually, no. I was told your grandma was here, and I need to talk with her." Anna Mae doesn't hide the shock on her face, so I turn to her grandma. "Mrs. Willow, may I have the honor of taking you to lunch? I have something to discuss that will be of great interest to you."

"Oh, posh, Royce. You sound like a used car salesman." Then, she levels me with her stare, "You're buying lunch?"

"Of course, I am." I know I have her now. She won't turn down a free meal.

"Well, I guess I can hear you out. Let's go." She finishes at the counter, and then takes my arm, as we walk extra slow down Main Street to the diner. I know she wants everyone to see her on my arm, so they wonder what we are doing. As much as she likes to share gossip, she likes to be the center of it, too. It's like a sport to these ladies.

As we enter the diner, all eyes turn on us, and Mrs. Willow struts in on my arm with a huge smile. She even picks a seat where we are in view of everyone else, but we can also talk without being overheard. I can give it to her because she knows exactly what we are doing.

Jo comes over and takes our order, and then Mrs. Willow turns to me. "Okay, spill it, young man. I know we aren't here for my good looks." She winks at me, and a big smile crosses my face.

"No, we aren't. I'm going to be level with you. I like Anna Mae. Really like her. I know her story, not all the details, but enough, and I understand why she's holding me at arm's length. So, that's where you come in."

Mrs. Willow places both hands under her chin and leans in to look at me. Her face gives nothing away, so I continue.

"Do you like Las Vegas, Mrs. Willow?"

"Do I like Las Vegas? Boy! Any time I can sit in an Elvis concert at night, and play some slots all morning, and stare at them pool boys all day, it's heaven. Some of the church ladies and I go once a year. Why?"

I chose to not point out how many sins she and the church ladies are committing in Sin City. I'm sure God turns the other cheek with all the good they do in town every year.

"Well, Maggie and Nick just got engaged, and they're doing a joint bachelor party in Las Vegas and are debating even getting married there, even though, Mom and Dad don't know that yet. Well, I was hoping you'd be willing to come with me, so we can convince Anna Mae to come along. I think a few days away relaxing might work in my favor. Heck, I'm up to try anything at this point."

Jo walks over and sets our food down, and we start eating in silence. I figure she's working out the details in her head, and I should let it be. A few bites into her cheeseburger, she finally speaks.

"I'm in, and I know I can get Anna Mae to go along with it. You haven't backed down, and I like that. It will take a lot more to win over my Anna Mae's heart. That devil of an ex-husband of hers chewed her heart up, spit it out, and did some kind of voodoo dance on it. I want to beat him to death with my cane, and I will if he ever thinks of stepping foot in Rock Springs!"

I grin at that one. I'm on Mrs. Willow's side. I'm sure I'd do a lot worse, and I don't even know the whole story. All I know is he cheated on her and left. I know there is more to it than that, but she doesn't want to talk about it, and I don't push. Any time her ex is brought up, she closes off again, and I'm tired of the hot and cold with her, so I'm willing to pull out the big guns.

"You let me talk to her, and I'll call you tonight, once I get her to agree." Mrs. Willow says. "And don't you be no snitch either. What happens in Vegas stays in Vegas. You let me spin my own tales when we get home."

She levels me with her 'or else' glare.

I nod my head in agreement, and we finish up our lunch, as she relays all the beauty shop gossip to me. Pastor Greg went out with a girl from Dallas, and it didn't go too well. Of course, what did he expect dating some city girl, right? I agree, and she keeps talking. The center of the gossip seems to be this illegal rodeo and talk of a few horses that have gone missing in the last week. Everyone hopes they catch these guys and fast because it has everyone in town on edge.

After lunch, I walk Mrs. Willow back to her car, and just like on the way here, she walks slowly, and even stops to window shop at a few stores to ensure we're seen. I make a note to ask Ella what story she tells in a few days.

On the way home, I start daydreaming of my time with Anna Mae in Las Vegas. I make myself a promise that if Mrs. Willow can get her to agree to go, I will take her to one of the Elvis shows and get her the best seats in the house.

I walk into the house, and Maggie and Ella are on the living room couch with bridal magazines spread out around them. I sit in the recliner, and they both look at me at the same time.

"Did you talk to Anna Mae?" Maggie asks.

"I did one better, I talked Mrs. Willow into going. She's going to talk Anna Mae into it for me. It's much harder for her to tell her grandma no than to tell me no."

Both my sisters bust out laughing. "You both aren't going to know what hit you. We have a plan, don't you worry." Ella winks at me.

"Ella no. None of that matchmaking stuff. Anna Mae isn't like you girls. She has been burned hard in the past, and earning her trust, is a slow process. Please, don't do anything to mess that up for me."

Ella holds her hands up in surrender, "I promise nothing to break her trust."

I glare at her, that's not a no matchmaking promise, but before I can go off on her, my phone pings.

Mrs. Willow: She said yes! Vegas here we come!

• • • ● • ● • • ·

Want Anna Mae and Royce's story? Make sure to grab **The Cowboy and His Vegas Wedding**!

Connect with Kaci M. Rose

Kaci M. Rose writes steamy small town cowboys. She also writes under Kaci Rose and there she writes wounded military heroes, giant mountain men, sexy rock stars, and even more there. Connect with her below!

Website
Facebook
Kaci Rose Reader's Facebook Group
Goodreads
Book Bub
Join Kaci M. Rose's VIP List (Newsletter)

More Books by Kaci M. Rose

Rock Springs Texas Series
The Cowboy and His Runaway – Blaze and Riley
The Cowboy and His Best Friend – Sage and Colt
The Cowboy and His Obsession – Megan and Hunter
The Cowboy and His Sweetheart – Jason and Ella
The Cowboy and His Secret – Mac and Sarah
Rock Springs Weddings Novella
Rock Springs Box Set 1-5 + Bonus Content

Cowboys of Rock Springs
The Cowboy and His Mistletoe Kiss – Lilly and Mike
The Cowboy and His Valentine – Maggie and Nick
The Cowboy and His Vegas Wedding – Royce and Anna

The Cowboy and His Angel – Abby and Greg
The Cowboy and His Christmas Rockstar – Savannah and Ford
The Cowboy and His Billionaire – Brice and Kayla

Walker Lake, Texas
The Cowboy and His Beauty - Sky and Dash

About Kaci M Rose

Kaci M Rose writes cowboy, hot and steamy cowboys set in all town anywhere you can find a cowboy.

She enjoys horseback riding and attending a rodeo where is always looking for inspiration.

Kaci grew on a small farm/ranch in Florida where they raised cattle and an orange grove. She learned to ride a four-wheeler instead of a bike (and to this day still can't ride a bike) and was driving a tractor before she could drive a car.

Kaci prefers the country to the city to this day and is working to buy her own slice of land in the next year or two!
Kaci M Rose is the Cowboy Romance alter ego of Author Kaci Rose.
See all of Kaci Rose's Books here.

Please Leave a Review!

I love to hear from my readers! Please **head over to your favorite store and leave a review** of what you thought of this book!

CPSIA information can be obtained
at www.ICGtesting.com
Printed in the USA
LVHW081106180822
726291LV00016B/278